SUGAR BASTARD

SUGAR DADDIES #6

CHARITY PARKERSON

Sugar Bastard
Sugar Daddies #6
Charity Parkerson

--Warning: This book is intended for readers over the age of 18.

Editor: BZ Hercules & Consultants

ISBN-13: 978-1-946099-38-9

ISBN-10: 1-946099-38-4

❀ Created with Vellum

INTRODUCTION

MEETING OMEN WAS LIKE A DREAM COME TRUE FOR KEEGAN. UNTIL HE FELL IN LOVE. THEN IT WAS A NIGHTMARE.

It had always been one of Keegan's secret fantasies to meet his favorite band, Slight Bastards. When it happened by complete accident, Keegan couldn't believe his luck. Then he found himself the center of the lead singer, Omen's, attention, and everything felt like a dream. Loving Omen came so easily. That is, until Omen made Keegan hate him.

The first time Omen set eyes on Keegan, he was caught. Keegan's stunning beauty confused Omen in a way he'd never expected. Before Keegan, Omen hadn't dated men. If he'd found one in his bed during a multi-person adventure, he hadn't balked, but one-on-one, Omen never thought it would be his thing. He doesn't want to start now, except he can't stay away. Falling in love with Keegan was easy. Being in love with him is the hardest thing Omen has ever faced. That is, until he watches Keegan's love turn to hate.

Omen doesn't know how to fix the damage he's done. Luckily, his friends have a plan. Now all it will take is everything if Omen hopes to win back his heart, but is it too late?

ONE

Two months of planning was finally coming to fruition. Since meeting Detroit in Vegas and spending the past eight weeks texting with the man, Keegan couldn't wait to drop the news now that his reservations were made. The first moment he had to pull out his phone, he sent a quick message off to Detroit.

Keegan: *What are you doing March 5th?*

Detroit: *Micah and his husband Wyld are throwing a huge fundraising event to raise money for their tiny home project. Their program moves the homeless into a tiny home community and sets them on a path to reclaiming their lives. I told Micah I'd help.*

Keegan: *That's awesome. What does the event entail?*

Detroit: *I believe there will be a walk to raise money. A play area for kids. Some games and booths. I think maybe some celebrity appearances. Things of that nature.*

Keegan: *Does he still need volunteers?*

Detroit: *Yes. It takes a ton of people to pull off something this huge.*

Keegan: *Awesome! I'm coming to town that weekend. Sign me up.*

The phone rang in Keegan's hand, startling him. He answered after a second of juggling. "Are you fucking kidding me? Don't toy with me. Are you really coming to see me?"

Detroit sounded genuinely happy. The thought fueled Keegan's excitement. A happy laugh escaped him. "Yes, I'm really coming. I know you'll be busy, but like I said, you can sign me up. I'll paint kids' faces or something."

"You'd be great at that."

"Meh," Keegan said, uncaring. "Probably not, since I'm not good with kids, but I'd get to see you and meet all the friends you're always telling me about." Keegan was ridiculously excited about meeting Detroit's friends. Since he'd met Detroit in

Vegas, under horrible circumstances, they'd become fast friends. Even though they practically lived on opposite ends of the country, Keegan felt closer to Detroit than he did anyone in New Orleans. That seemed odd since Keegan had met Detroit after he'd caught Detroit kissing his ex—the one who still owned Keegan's heart.

"What day are you coming in? Would you like to stay with me? We have the room."

A laugh escaped Keegan at Detroit's influx of questions. "I'm coming in on the fifth and I'm staying two weeks. Since I've never been to California, I decided I wanted to stay on the beach, so I booked a room with a view, but I promise to spend as much time with you as your husband will spare." Detroit was newlywed and Keegan didn't want to intrude.

"Which hotel?"

"The Luna. You said you fight there, so I thought it would be the easiest place if I hope to also catch a match while in town."

"This is so awesome," Detroit cheered, sounding every bit as happy as Keegan felt. "Who's watching the store while you're out?"

Keegan loved that Detroit worried over every detail. He didn't have much of that in his life. "This is my slow season, so I'm closing up for two weeks.

You know I can't trust my family to watch the place. They'll be all up in my apartment, searching through my stuff. I'm saving all that for after I'm dead, so I won't be embarrassed."

"I'm paying someone in advance to just burn my house down when I die," Detroit said with a laugh. "That's better for everyone involved."

Keegan's smile made his face hurt. Maybe it was crazy to feel so close to someone he hadn't known for long, but Detroit made it easy. "I miss your face." His throat swelled as he made the claim. He hadn't realized until he heard Detroit's voice how much he'd come to care about the man.

"Same here, but I know as soon as I introduce you to everyone, they'll steal you away."

Detroit always warmed his heart because he never failed to treat Keegan like he was normal, and people would love him. That wasn't at all the case. In fact, in his experience, most people did not like him. It wasn't that he didn't try. Keegan was simply unapologetically himself. Detroit began reciting a long list of people he intended to ensure Keegan met while there. Keegan listened to the cadence of the man's voice more than his words. He hoped like hell this vacation brought him a sense of peace that had eluded him since losing Omen five months earlier.

4

Keegan stared out the window of his shop. The sunshine was near to blinding. He wondered what the weather was like where Omen was today. Maybe it was night there. He no longer knew where Keegan was each day. As the lead singer for Slight Bastards, a popular metal band, Omen had been on tour for almost a year. Keegan had stopped keeping track of the band's every stop, hoping to hang on to his sanity. Maybe that ship had sailed a long time ago. Keegan hadn't felt the least bit sane since meeting Omen. It was possible his heart and mind had stopped doing anything beyond keeping his body alive. Fuck if he knew how to check. Maybe he'd died, and no one had told him. Life had felt a lot like hell lately.

OMEN SWITCHED his attention between writing a new song and eating. Occasionally, his gaze would stray to the window of the café he'd found down the street from his hotel. So far, in the past week, no one had bothered him here. One waitress had asked for his autograph, but otherwise, he'd been left to eat and write in peace. It was a rare occurrence, especially when he was on tour. In his hometown of New Orleans, he was pretty much left alone, but people were used to seeing him there. The only time he found himself swarmed by fans back home was after a concert when people came from miles around to see him.

Rain covered the streets, making the street lights come on hours early. For some reason, the phenomenon always fascinated him. It relaxed him when it looked like night during the day. During hurricane season back home, it rained a lot. He used to spend days like this in bed with Keegan. As the man's name floated through his mind, Omen rubbed his chest. There were so many miles and issues sitting between them. The blame sat squarely on Omen's shoulders. He couldn't deny it, and it was a hard pill to swallow. Five months earlier, after over a year of being together, Keegan had rightfully gotten sick of being kept a secret and walked away. There hadn't been any huge drama. There never was with Keegan. He genuinely had simply left Omen standing in the street, gotten in a cab, and never contacted Omen again. That is, until two months ago when he'd shown up in Vegas and caught Omen kissing Detroit. What a fucked-up mess Omen had made of his life. He wished he could blame someone else. Unfortunately, it was all him. He hadn't wanted a label. Being with Keegan in the eyes of the world would give him one he'd never escape. He was so fucking stupid. The longer Omen thought about Keegan, the darker his thoughts went. His phone buzzed, crawling across the table and saving him from himself.

As if thinking about that kiss with Detroit conjured him, Omen spotted Detroit's name on his phone. He didn't hesitate to answer. Any distraction at all was a life line he couldn't ignore.

"Hello?"

"Dude, what are you doing March the fifth?"

Detroit's enthusiasm pulled a laugh from Omen. "Well, hello to you too, Detroit. I'm fine. How are you?"

Detroit huffed. Omen bit back another laugh. "That's good. I'm great. Now, what are you doing March the fifth?"

"I'd have to check my calendar, but off-hand, I'd say nothing. Why?" Omen took a sip of his drink while he waited for Detroit to get to the point.

"Well," Detroit said, dragging out the word. "You know my friend Micah?"

"I know of him." Omen relished interrupting Detroit. He knew it had been a rhetorical question. He just kind of liked annoying Detroit.

"Anyhow," Detroit said, talking over him. "He's

putting together this huge charity event for his back-to-work and tiny home program. It's this thing he started that helps the homeless get jobs, housing, and their lives back on track. There's a few bands already signed up to perform. Would you like to add your name?"

"Honestly, that's something my agent usually handles."

"I ask because Keegan is coming for two weeks and has already agreed to volunteer at the event."

At Detroit's interruption, Omen's heart raced into his throat. "Yes. I'm there."

Detroit's voice turned smug. "Are you sure you don't want me to contact your agent?"

Omen bit back a growl. "I'll take care of it. I'm there." He was wrapping up an international tour and hadn't been back home yet. It had been Omen's intent to lay siege to Keegan's life once they were in the same town, but that was weeks away. If Detroit could get them on the same turf for even five minutes, Omen wanted it.

TWO

EVEN THOUGH DETROIT ACCEPTED KEEGAN'S decision to stay in a hotel with grace, he staunchly refused to let Keegan take a cab from the airport. Since then, his life had passed in a blur of unreality. He'd been whisked to breakfast. Met the man's ridiculously sexy husband. Not jealous at all. Stopped by the hotel only long enough to drop his bags. Now he was as standing at the door of what he'd been told was a house, but yeah. He didn't believe it. It was like a mega-mansion. Not that Keegan had anything to compare the place to. He lived in a tiny apartment. Even Omen, who had tons of money, didn't own a place like this. Keegan couldn't stop tugging on his clothes. Out of place didn't begin to describe his current mood.

"Why do I suddenly feel underdressed?" Keegan asked, eyeing the multi-million-dollar home.

Detroit chuckled. The sound—like the man—was hot. It was wrong for someone who already looked like a superhero to be so perfect in every way. Sickening really. Keegan should hate him, but he couldn't. "Don't worry. Micah is married to Wyld West. Wyld might have more money than God, but he... well, you'll just have to see for yourself."

"I don't know who that is," Keegan muttered under his breath.

A tall, slender guy with pale skin and amber-colored eyes answered the door. Dressed all in black, he looked perfectly pressed and untouchable. His gaze swept over them.

"Hey, Cortland," Detroit said, sounding bright, as if the guy didn't look unwelcoming.

"Micah's in the kitchen." His gaze slid Keegan's way. "I'm Cortland."

Keegan smiled, pouring on the southern charm. "I'm Keegan. It's nice to meet you."

Cortland softened. Sort of. His mouth twitched a little as he stepped aside, letting them in. "Detroit tells me you're interested in helping out today," Cortland said as he led Keegan through the house. "Micah's thrilled to have you."

10

"I work a lot, so I don't get much time to volunteer. Since I'm here and on vacation, I figured I'd do what I could." As the words finished leaving his lips, the kitchen came into view. So too did the most beautifully angelic-looking man Keegan had ever set eyes upon. His blond curls begged to be touched. The man smiled as he greeted Detroit. His gaze swung Keegan's way and Keegan fought a sigh.

"Is this Keegan?"

At his question, Detroit nodded. "Micah, this is Keegan Bordelon. Keegan, this is Micah West. Micah's been begging for an introduction since we met."

Micah came to his feet. He swatted Detroit's arm but directed his words at Keegan. "I've been best friends with this ass since I was fourteen. Whenever he makes a new friend, I want in too. You're even more gorgeous than he described. Truly, I'm thinking I should throw you out before my husband sees you."

A nervous laugh rose in Keegan's throat, and then Micah hugged him. Warmth filled Keegan's chest. He wanted to hold on. For some reason, he felt blessed. "I've been ridiculously excited to meet you too." Keegan pushed the words past his tight throat. "I'm glad I chose a time to visit when I can also help out." Something moved behind Micah, catching

Keegan's eye. A tiny dog, even smaller than the shoe he was shitting in, captured Keegan's attention. "Um, there's a dog shitting in a shoe over there."

A loud sigh escaped Micah. He glanced over his shoulder. "Baby," he called, sounding tired. "We'll have to give Cortland another raise."

At his announcement, Cortland cursed and went after the dog. Another man appeared in the doorway. He was shirtless and sexy in a carefree way. "What's happened?" And, damn, he had a British accent.

"Bear just ruined another one of his shoes," Micah explained before motioning Keegan's way. "This is Keegan, Detroit's friend who's in town on vacation. He's volunteered to help us out today. Keegan, this is my husband, Wyld."

"Charmed," Wyld said, barely sparing him a glance. Instead, he watched Cortland scolding the tiny puppy, who didn't seem to care. "It's your fault," Wyld said, obviously unsympathetic as he moved to intercede and rescue the dog. Bear transformed before Keegan's eyes, turning sweet and shamelessly kissing ass as he snuggled against Wyld's chest. "See? He knows you're a no-good cheat. You go to Driver's and come back smelling like his dog. If Micah came home smelling like another man, I'd shit in his shoes too, so really, you had it coming."

Micah shot a disbelieving look Wyld's way. "Did you just..." He shook his head. "Never mind. I know you too well. You probably would shit in my shoes."

At the surety in Micah's tone, Keegan laughed. He couldn't help it. They were adorable.

Wyld crossed the room and captured Micah's lips in a kiss so blatantly sexual Keegan felt like he should be paying to watch. Still, he didn't look away. They were... wow. The only thing stopping Keegan from getting steamy was watching Bear. The tiny brown dog that looked exactly like a teddy bear was visibly torn. He tried snuggling with both men—like they were pressed together for his sole benefit. It was the cutest thing Keegan had ever seen.

"You have company," Cortland said, sounding bored.

"My house," Wyld said, pulling away enough to brush noses with Micah. "Oh, sexy, if you ever cheated on me, I'd tie you to the bed until you begged to stay with me. Then I'd have the other man killed. I can afford at least one murder."

"People can see you," Cortland said, trying again.

"I'm not offended. Keep going." A hint of horror crept in as Keegan heard his needy tone. Still, he couldn't stop his mouth. "Sorry. I've been single for..." He tried calculating in his head. "I don't want to think about that."

Wyld winked. "Don't apologize. You'll learn quick that I'm ridiculously in love with my angel. He doesn't get much peace."

The endearment struck Keegan. Micah did look exactly like an angel.

"I'd throw in my two cents here, but it feels odd now that I'm Micah's stepdad."

Detroit's claim brought Keegan up short. "You are?"

Micah's gaze finally moved from his husband like a spell had broken. "Yeah. You didn't know Detroit is married to my dad?"

"Everyone here is so scandalous," Wyld said, sounding like an old school marm. He tried covering Bear's eyes. "Don't look, baby. Mommy will save you from the perverts."

"Jesus," Cortland muttered, sidling up next to Keegan. "Are you sure you're ready for this day? I can hide you if you'd like. I know all the best spots. That's the only way I've survived years of living with and working for Wyld."

Even though Cortland seemed more serious than the rest, Keegan felt an immediate kinship with him. There was something about him. He obviously didn't wear his feelings on his sleeve. Keegan got the impression he was still waters, and he liked deep people. It was why he'd fallen for Omen and his poetic soul.

Keegan flashed the man a grateful smile. "I might take you up on that," he said in a low voice, hoping not to offend anyone. "I'm not used to a lot of busyness."

Cortland eyed him for a moment. "I know the perfect person to pair you with today. His name is Driver. He used to be homeless, but Micah's program helped him get back on his feet and now he works as one of the program leaders. You'll like him. He's quiet."

"Is this the same Driver who has Bear shitting in your shoes?"

A smile lit Cortland's face. The gesture transformed him. He had dimples, but not just any dimples. Cortland had the little adorable indentions that appeared beneath his eyes. He looked younger and kind of breathtaking. "Yeah, you're definitely not going to want to come back here after meeting him. Bear won't thank you."

"Well, you only live once." Not to mention, the more people Detroit introduced him to, the more comfortable Keegan became. People didn't make a point of getting to know him. The fact that he wore makeup and liked women's clothes made people leery. He was odd, even by New Orleans standards. Since landing in California, Keegan hadn't felt this accepted in his whole life.

CORTLAND WAS RIGHT ABOUT DRIVER. The man was quiet and brooding. They'd spent hours together, setting up the children's area for the event. Keegan felt like he could breathe. There was no pressure to smile or make small talk. It was nice. Tying ribbons to the end of balloons wasn't thrilling work. Keegan's mind wandered too much. After several minutes of glancing around the room, Keegan found something to occupy his brain. Cortland watched Driver like the man was his next meal. It wasn't super obvious, since Cortland wasn't a very animated person to begin with, but his gaze was hungry and lit while staring at Driver. There was passion inside Cortland.

Keegan switched his gaze to Driver, watching him on the sly. At some point, he'd repositioned his chair, facing the direction Cortland worked. Keegan's interest ratcheted up another notch.

Driver's gaze slid Cortland's way. He chewed his bottom lip. Keegan caught himself leaning closer. He was such a sucker for love.

"So, Cortland seems nice," Keegan said, incapable of not digging for more.

Driver's blue gaze collided with Keegan's. "Yeah. He does a lot for Micah's organization."

"It seems like it," Keegan agreed. "But I guess I didn't really mean it that way. I meant, he's nice in a friendly sort of way." Keegan wasn't good at weaseling secrets from people.

Driver looked Cortland's way again. His mouth lifted at the corners. "He's amazing. I don't know what I'd do without him. He's my best friend."

Keegan glanced Cortland's way. A wave of pity washed over him. It was obvious Cortland believed they were more than friends, or he wanted to be more. Either way, it hurt like hell to be reduced to being just a friend. Keegan would know. He'd never forget the day Omen had finally broken him with those same words.

Omen went from smiling to closed in an instant. He stepped away from Keegan, putting some distance between them as they walked.

"Omen. Oh my gosh. I didn't know you were in town."

Keegan's gaze followed the call, landing on an older woman. She had silver hair and more jewelry than any one person should wear. Her warm expression and the way she kissed Omen's cheek said she cared about Omen. Keegan kept smiling, waiting to be introduced.

"Hey, Mom. I just got in last night."

Oh, great. It was his mom, and he was lying. He'd been in Keegan's bed every night for two weeks. Still, Keegan kept a smile plastered on his face like his life depended upon it.

"I'd planned to come see you later, but this is great. It's like we were meant to run into each other."

Her gaze slid Keegan's way and stayed, leaving Omen no choice but to introduce them.

"Keegan, this is my mom, Nancy."

"Mom, this is my best friend, Keegan."

Keegan's stomach dropped at the introduction. It didn't help that Omen's mom was looking at him like he was a freak.

"You Hollywood types and your makeup. I'll never understand it."

"I'm from here," Keegan muttered, but he'd already been dismissed and forgotten. Omen's mom was going on about some third cousin removed who'd passed. Keegan's insides churned with hurt and

anger. There was a cab sitting at the corner. Keegan didn't let himself think. He simply walked away, jumped inside, and gave his address. His gaze stayed glued to the windshield. He wouldn't let himself look back. Keegan kept the pain tightly held to his chest. The move made it hard to breathe, but he'd been choking for months now, suffocating beneath Omen's denial. There was a tiny part of him that twinged at having been rude to Omen's mom by walking away. His mother had taught him better. But he'd never see her again. He'd also never see Omen again. That was crippling, but it was time. They were over.

"Is he really your best friend?" Keegan asked Driver before he could stop himself.

Driver's face screwed up in obvious confusion. He glanced at Cortland again and back at Keegan. "What?"

Keegan waved his hand dismissively. "Sorry. It's just you two don't look at each other like friends. I wondered if you were just saying that because you didn't want to admit it's more or because it's true?"

Driver's features closed. "I don't know what you mean."

"Okay," Keegan said, dragging out the word. "Well, from an outsider's point of view, you're always looking at him when he isn't looking. He's always looking at you when you're not looking. Then you both do that thing where you quickly look away when you get caught. It's kind of adorable. Unless you're lying about how you feel. There's nothing cute about being a liar." Yeah, he was projecting, but also, he was telling the truth. No one liked being kept a secret. It broke people in a way that couldn't be repaired.

Driver blinked. "He looks at me when I'm not looking?"

Okay, it was adorable. "Constantly."

Driver shook his head as if refusing to let any ideas take root. "It doesn't matter. He's too good for me. I have literally nothing to offer. His friendship is enough."

An ugly-sounding snort escaped Keegan before he could call it back. "I've seen where he lives. He doesn't need you to have anything to offer other than yourself. Stop overthinking things."

Driver shrugged and went back to filling balloons. "It is what it is."

Keegan went back to tying on the ribbon, letting it drop. It wasn't his business, and he didn't have any right to dole out advice. His shit hadn't been together in years.

"You now know my biggest secret. Tell me about

yourself," Driver said, changing the subject and obviously uncomfortable with silence.

Keegan flashed him a bright smile. He wasn't above talking about himself. "I own a vintage dress shop in the heart of New Orleans."

"You seem awful young to own your own business." Driver didn't sound insulting, more like he was curious.

"It belonged to my grandmother," Keegan explained. "I've worked there since I was big enough to reach the cash register. She left the place to me when she died three years ago. The rest of the family wasn't thrilled, but I'm the one who worked from sun up to sundown with her, making the place profitable. Luckily, the location does the heavy lifting. There's always some type of ball or party going on in NOLA requiring costumes, and I'm the only real game in town." Keegan shrugged, watching his hands and tying balloons. "I'm not getting rich or anything, but I like it. Plus, it has a small apartment upstairs, so I don't have to pay for housing."

"I've always wanted to go to New Orleans. Obviously, I haven't had the funds."

"Well," Keegan said, concentrating on his work. "If you ever get the chance, I'm in a great tourist location and I have a spare room."

"You don't know me," Driver said, sounding so serious and deadly Keegan met his stare. Driver held his gaze. His blue eyes looked hard. "You're too nice. Don't invite strangers into your home."

Keegan winked, hoping to diffuse whatever he'd done wrong. "It's a southern thing. We're always like —you can stay with me, knowing our invitation will never be accepted. Am I wrong, or did you intend to take me up on my offer?"

A chuckle escaped Driver. His features transformed. "No. I wouldn't have accepted."

"Do you think we have enough balloons?" Keegan asked, eyeing the ceiling. "If we keep this up, I'm afraid the wind will carry me away when I take them outside."

"I'd save you."

Keegan's entire body seized at the quietly spoken words at his back. He'd know Omen's voice anywhere. He still heard the man in his dreams. Driver's gaze moved from a spot over Keegan's shoulder to Keegan's face. He looked concerned, making Keegan wonder what the man saw in his expression. Probably his instant desire to burst into tears. Keegan stood. He refused to look Omen's way as he gathered the balloons. His heart rate kicked up.

Oxygen refused to reach his brain. He blinked, trying to fight the burning behind his eyes.

Omen moved closer. "Let me help."

Driver shot to his feet and grabbed the balloons before Omen could. "We've got this. If you're looking to volunteer, go see Cortland over there. He'll get you assigned to something."

Keegan kept his gaze locked on Driver and prayed he wouldn't fall apart.

Of course, Omen didn't simply give up and walk away. "Keegan."

Keegan's eyes fell closed at the sound of his name on Omen's lips. The pain was more than he could bear. "Excuse me," he gasped through a tightened throat, leaving Driver to deal with the balloons alone. Without waiting for anyone's response, he walked at a fast clip toward the door. He'd volunteered to be here, and he'd do his part, but not this second. Right now, he needed distance. Otherwise, there was a real chance he'd snap.

Once he hit the back door, Keegan closed his eyes and sucked in a deep breath. The smell of the ocean hit him. His eyes opened. The sun was reflecting off the water. Time slipped away.

The bell chimed above the door, reminding Keegan he'd forgotten to lock it. "I'm sorry. We're closed," he called out as he headed toward the front of the shop.

"Oh, good. Does that mean I can lock this?" the stranger asked as he turned the lock on the door. A shot of fear ran through Keegan while a mob of people ran past the door, screaming. He hoped like hell some criminal hadn't just locked himself inside Keegan's shop.

"What's going on out there? Do I need to call the cops?"

"No, I—" the man said as he turned. His long blond hair and tall frame nearly had Keegan swallowing his tongue. He knew that face.

"You're Omen Birch," Keegan said, interrupting him and incapable of stopping the words. He couldn't believe it. Omen Birch, the leader singer of Keegan's favorite band was there—inside his shop, hiding from screaming fans.

Omen's eyes, which were even better in real life, were locked on Keegan. The green reflected the light, nearly making Keegan sigh. "Is it okay if I hang out while the crowd dies down? Usually, it's not like this."

"Of course. I mean, I was about to head upstairs, but I can't throw you out to the wolves."

"Upstairs sounds great. Less chance of anyone

seeing me through the window," he added, sounding uncomfortable.

Normally, Keegan wouldn't invite a stranger upstairs, but it was Omen Birch. He couldn't say no. Even if he turned up dead, what a way to go. "Come on," Keegan said, motioning him toward the back where the stairs to his apartment were located. "I'll make you some tea."

"Thanks, but I'm not really a tea drinker. You have some really amazing ink."

Keegan thanked every deity his back was turned to Omen. Heat exploded in his cheeks. "Thanks. The tattoo artist I use is an award-winning artist. He does tours and stuff, but he just moved to Phoenix, so I'll probably stop where I'm at. Plus, my mom worries she won't recognize me anymore soon." Keegan had no idea why he couldn't stop babbling bullshit. The man had simply complimented his tattoos, and Keegan was ready to spill his life story. Keegan opened the door to his apartment and waved Omen inside. Omen was so freaking tall. Keegan felt tiny as he passed.

"I'm a weakling," Omen said as he stood in the center of Keegan's living room, eyeing everything. "Going under the needle scares me."

Keegan shrugged as he set his keys and phone on the side table by the door. The move caused his boat neck shirt to slide down and expose one shoulder. "Getting inked is not for everyone. I like art and bright colors. As soon as I was old enough to start painting my body, I did." He met Omen's gaze. "If you don't like tea, what would you like to drink?"

Omen waved off his question. "Don't worry over me. I get that you're just getting off work. Do what you need to do and pretend I'm not here."

A smile that felt out of control, even to him, lit Keegan's face. "This is surreal as hell. I have a rock star in my apartment and you want me to pretend you're not here."

Omen nodded. His light green eyes mesmerized Keegan. "I like it when you're not looking at me. That way I can stare at you on the sly."

Another blush hit Keegan without warning. "It's not on the sly if you tell me you're doing it."

"I'm sorry. I don't mean to stare."

Keegan pushed a stray hair behind his ear. Butterflies stirred in his stomach. He couldn't remember the last time he was this nervous. "It's okay. People stare at me all the time, trying to figure me out. It's the makeup and the women's clothes," Keegan admitted. "And me," he couldn't help but tack on, feeling subconscious.

Omen shook his head. "That's not why I'm

staring. You're stunning—like the sunset reflecting on the ocean. I can't tear my eyes away."

Keegan pressed a hand to his stomach, trying to fight back the tidal wave of pain. He was different from other people. Keegan had been fine with himself before Omen. He'd been okay with knowing he might never find anyone who understood and loved him. Then, Omen had shown up, and for the first time in his life, he'd felt ashamed of how he looked and his inability to change. Now here Omen was—poised to completely wreck Keegan again. No one understood what it was like, loving someone who was embarrassed to love them back. Just knowing Omen was feet away made Keegan want to cry and cry until he had nothing left. The funny thing was, he thought he'd already done that for Omen.

"Are you okay?"

Keegan's head snapped around at the intrusion. It was Driver. Keegan drew a deep breath. "Yes. No. It doesn't matter," he said, flashing Driver a pained smile.

"Are you afraid of that guy?"

Driver's obvious concern warmed Keegan's heart and made him feel like shit for running away. "No." It was lie, of course. Keegan was scared shitless of what Omen could do to his heart. "He was my best friend, once upon a time," Keegan explained.

Driver turned his head and focused on the water. The light caressed his features, highlighting his muscular jaw and blue eyes. He understood what Cortland saw in the man. Driver was hard and a little scary—like he might be protective or dangerous. Everyone loved that toxic combination.

"Was he really your best friend?" Driver asked without looking his way.

Despite the pains in his chest, a smile pulled at Keegan's lips. "That's what he told everyone who asked. You should go back inside and tell Cortland how you feel."

"No offense, but from where I stand, that hasn't worked out so well for you."

Keegan had nothing. Omen's presence had wiped him clean.

Driver shook his head. "I'm sorry. I shouldn't have said that."

"No," Keegan said, cutting off his apology. "You're right. I don't know you and you don't know me. Obviously, I have no right to give advice. My life sucks. It's a horrible mess. Do what you want."

Driver opened his mouth. What he intended to

say, Keegan would never know. Detroit appeared, cutting him off.

"Are you all right?"

Driver walked away without saying a word. Keegan felt like shit. This was why he had no friends. He swallowed, trying to bury the anger and pain. This was supposed to be his vacation. Everything sucked. "I guess you knew when you asked me to volunteer that he would be here. Thanks for that. Next time, I'll stick closer to home."

The guilt in Detroit's expression said Keegan had hit the nail on the head with his accusations. "You love each other. What could it hurt to talk to him?"

Rage owned Keegan. "Are you fucking kidding me? Everything, Detroit. It hurts every fucking thing inside of me to see his face. Hear his voice. His existence breaks me. I know you don't get that. It's more than obvious no one has ever been ashamed of you. Everyone is always ashamed of me. He was the only time it mattered. Do you get that this was a really shitty thing to do?"

"I just want you to be happy," Detroit said, sounding genuinely upset. "Honest to God, I believe Omen let people get pictures of us together so no one would bat an eye when he's seen with you. He's trying."

Keegan shook his head. He should've known better than to cling to a friendship with someone who was also friends with Omen. In the end, if the choice was between them, no one ever chose Keegan. "I promised I would help today, so I will. Otherwise, please stay away from me."

The flash of hurt that crossed Detroit's gorgeous features made Keegan instantly regret the words. He couldn't take them back. As much as he understood that Detroit had been trying to help, Detroit didn't understand. Everyone loved him. He couldn't know what life was like for Keegan. Clutching his hurt to his chest, Keegan walked away. Maybe he'd be over this later, but not today. Today, he needed space.

OMEN STARED at the door Keegan and Detroit disappeared through for so long without blinking his eyes burned. Part of him wanted to chase Keegan down. Make him listen. His feet wouldn't budge. Each time he saw Keegan, the pain choked the life from him. He'd fallen in love so easily with Keegan, but there'd been nothing easy about loving Keegan.

"Why don't you ditch the makeup for one day? Just throw on some jeans and a t-shirt and let's go to lunch."

Keegan turned away from the mirror. Half his makeup was already done. A smile stretched his lips. "You act like you've been waiting forever. I'm almost done."

Omen's skin itched. He was restless in a way he couldn't explain. They'd been in public enough times that Omen already knew how this would go. He'd keep his chair far enough away so he wouldn't be tempted to reach for Keegan. There'd be a mental count in his head, ensuring he didn't stare longer than five seconds. He'd keep his sunglasses on inside, hiding the emotions he couldn't without them. Mental torture. That was what going out meant. Omen's feet moved without his permission. He snagged Keegan around the middle from behind, hauling him away from the bathroom mirror.

"I've changed my mind. We're staying in. I'll call someone and get our food delivered."

Peals of laughter escaped Keegan as Omen dragged him toward the bed. "No, Omen. I spent all this time on my face."

"Nope," Omen cried, pulling out his loud whine.

"I'm not sharing you with the world today. You're mine. Do you hear me? Mine."

Keegan's chest heaved as he visibly tried catching his breath between laughs after Omen tossed him onto the bed. He tried springing back to his feet. Omen covered Keegan's body with his before the man could get away.

"Omen," Keegan said, sounding out of breath as he pushed at Omen's chest. "You promised me food."

"You'll get it." He dragged Keegan's shirt up as he made the claim. "After you take off all your clothes, I swear I'll call for takeout." He dipped his head and nuzzled Keegan's neck. "Come on, baby. Play with me. Let's stay in bed today."

Keegan blew out a loud breath. "An hour ago, you couldn't wait to get out of here."

Omen settled in, keeping Keegan pinned to the bed. "That was an hour ago. I was feeling like an old man who can't keep up with you then. Now I'm rested and want to try again."

The way Keegan's gaze moved over his face let Omen know the truth was sinking in. Keegan's smile fell. Omen's throat tightened. He always did this. One day, Keegan would get up, leave, and never look back. Keegan's gaze skirted away. A pained look crossed his features. He cleared his throat. "Go order the food."

The dead note to Keegan's voice was a knife to the heart. Omen hated himself. He didn't know how to change. "I love you."

Keegan's gaze stayed locked elsewhere—like he couldn't even look at Omen. "I know."

Funny. Keegan's "I know" sounded a hell of a lot like he thought Omen was lying. Maybe he was. After all, if he really loved Keegan, he wouldn't treat him this way. Right?

Omen didn't deserve to chase after Keegan. He'd lost that privilege. Killed it a little more each time he'd chosen his reputation over Keegan's feelings. Yet, here he was—ready to destroy Keegan again. He couldn't stop. Omen was completely incapable of not trying to be with Keegan. Not loving him.

"Well, he hates me now," Detroit said, reappearing and pulling Omen from his bleak thoughts.

"I shouldn't have agreed to this." Omen took the blame for himself. "Don't worry. He won't stay mad at you for long. He's not good at holding on to anger. I'm the exception to that, but only because I hurt him too many times to be worthy of any more forgiveness."

Detroit's chest expanded as he took a deep

breath. Omen hated how upset he looked. "I'll give him some space and try talking to him again later."

Omen dropped his gaze to his feet. He'd known seeing Keegan wouldn't be easy. It was hard as hell to stay put and not chase after him. There were knives in his throat and ants living under his skin at the thought of Keegan never speaking to him again. He wanted to scream, rage, and throw shit. All Omen could do was stand there and let the slow hands on the clock tick by.

His space was invaded before he had time to react. Light blue eyes and rage bore down on him. The dark-haired man matched Omen in height. Not many people did. Omen recognized him as the guy who'd been helping Keegan earlier. The one who'd followed Keegan out. "Haven't you figured out yet you're not welcome?"

Detroit tried to intervene. "That's enough, Driver. Omen is my guest."

Driver's hard gaze slid Detroit's way. Omen almost took a step back, and he wasn't the one beneath the man's stare. This guy was dangerous. Omen didn't imagine many people fucked with Detroit. Driver wasn't scared. In fact, he was downright frightening. "Back away, Detroit." Without waiting for Detroit to comply, Driver's gaze shifted back to Omen. "I don't know your story, but Keegan doesn't want you here. That's enough for me."

"Is everything okay?" A skinny guy who looked like a strong wind might blow him over showed up to intercede. He brushed his hand down Driver's arm. Driver's entire body went on alert. Omen took that step back he'd been contemplating. He didn't think he'd ever met someone truly capable of murder. Omen didn't think he could make that same claim after today.

Driver looked away. "I could use your help to move all these balloons to the kid's area. Keegan needed a break." Driver didn't meet anyone's eye as he made the claim, but it was obvious the words were meant for the only guy brave enough to touch him.

"Sure," the new arrival said as he eyed each of them, visibly confused.

"Thanks, Cortland," Detroit said as he led Driver away.

"Well, fuck." Omen couldn't stop the muttered curse. As bad as he'd expected this day to be, it was topping a whole new level of bullshit. He had no one else to blame but himself.

"WOULD you like to tell me what just happened?"

Driver gathered several balloons without looking Cortland's way. "Nothing."

"I see."

Cortland was the only person Driver knew who could sound so proper and pissed at the same time. It wasn't that Driver didn't want to talk to Cortland. He didn't know how. Most people would take one look at Cortland and dismiss him as a snob. That wasn't true in the least. Driver had seen other men like him. Men who made it through the day by staying contained. Men who'd endured the unspeakable. In truth, they were a lot alike, except Cortland might break without his armor of polish while Driver might hurt someone without his tight lid. The long-haired douche who Driver had left behind had caused something to boil inside him, threatening his barely held grip on sanity. Cortland's silence wasn't helping. Driver could handle picking a fight and possibly landing in jail. Being given the silent treatment by Cortland was worse than the years he spent killing everyone his country ordered him to point his gun toward.

Driver ground his back teeth to a pulp. He lasted until they were outside. "That guy did something to Keegan."

Cortland glanced over. His serene mask slipped. "How do you mean?"

"Not physically," Driver said, rushing to explain. He hadn't thought before he'd spoken. "I mean, they used to be friends, but he did something that hurt Keegan. I'm not sure what." Driver shrugged. "Probably I shouldn't have gotten involved, but you should've seen Keegan's face when he showed up."

Cortland looked away. "Oh."

"What's that 'oh' for?" Sometimes, Driver didn't get Cortland. He always dug for more from Driver, but every time Driver opened up, Cortland retreated. "You asked what happened, and I explained."

Without meeting Driver's gaze, Cortland tied his set of balloons to a chair under the kids' awning. They'd hand them out later while Keegan painted faces. If Keegan came back, that is. "It's just, that was a pretty severe reaction you had in there over a guy you just met. I mean, Keegan is... I guess I... Never mind," Cortland said, sounding unusually frustrated. "I'll grab the rest of the balloons."

Driver snagged Cortland's arm before he could get away, leaving the man no other choice but to meet his gaze. Cortland's cheeks were flushed with silent anger. The light hit his eyes at just the right angle, making their unusual amber coloration almost unnaturally light. For a moment, Driver couldn't think straight. "Talk to me."

Cortland held his stare. His bravery was the sexiest thing Driver had ever seen. "Keegan is beautiful. I can't compete. You can let go of me now."

Driver ignored him. "Why would you want to compete?"

"I don't." The defiant set to Cortland's jaw fascinated Driver.

His hold on Cortland's arm transformed into a caress. "You should get the rest of the balloons."

Cortland's gaze dropped to Driver's mouth before quickly returning to hold his stare. "I'm trying."

"I don't want Keegan."

"Okay." Cortland sounded disbelieving.

Driver couldn't stop. "Someone else already has my attention."

"Oh."

The level of disappointment in that single word made Driver's chest hurt. "He's blind as hell, though."

Cortland tried shifting away. Driver refused to let him go. "I can't compete with a blind man either, or anyone, really."

Driver shook his head. "Damn, Cort. I know you're not this dumb."

"You'd be surprised."

With a tired-sounding sigh, Driver dropped Cortland's arm and looked away. It was for the best. Like he'd told Keegan, he didn't have anything to offer. "Get the rest of the balloons. I'll set up the face paints."

"Driver."

Driver forced himself to meet Cortland's stare. Disappointment ate at his gut. He worried there was no way he could hide it. "Did you need something else?"

Cortland chewed his bottom lip. His heart was in his eyes. Driver couldn't look away. To him, Cortland was the most gorgeous man on the planet, especially when he smiled. Driver wanted to make him smile. The distance between them disappeared. Driver didn't know which of them moved, but he was positive he was the one who pressed his lips to Cortland's. The air stuttered from his lungs when Cortland kissed him back. He'd spent too many nights fantasizing. Cortland's kiss was even better than he could've imagined. For a moment, Cortland's fingertips skimmed his jaw, as if he savored the moment. Then, Cortland backed away.

He looked slightly panicked. "You're too good for me." Cortland was serious. It was in his eyes. He meant every word. Driver's brain was still too addled from their kiss. He couldn't think. By the time he found any words, Cortland was gone, and Driver had no clue what happened.

THREE

KEEGAN KEPT A FAKE SMILE IN PLACE FOR SO long he thought his face would crack. For hours, he painted faces, chatted with parents and their kids, and handed out balloons. He did all this while trying not to make eye contact with Driver. Keegan hated feeling like an ass, and he double hated that he'd snapped at a man who'd only wanted to help. When the music began, the children's area cleared as everyone moved to listen to the various bands. Keegan kept a tight lid on his thoughts. He could feel them brewing beneath a flimsy layer of distraction. A familiar face caught his attention. Keegan's eyes burned. Even though he didn't understand his reaction, Keegan met Micah halfway as the man moved in his direction. Micah opened his arms and Keegan walked into his embrace, as if they'd known each other forever, and he'd known there was no better comfort.

His eyes fell closed as Micah's arms encircled him. The hurt rose to the surface. He was dangerously close to crying. Keegan needed Micah to leach the pain from him. For some reason, he knew the man could.

"I'm so sorry," Micah said, as if he had anything to apologize for. "I just heard what happened. Sometimes, Detroit doesn't think. His heart is always in the right place, but he doesn't truly consider how other people might feel."

"I feel ambushed."

Micah rubbed his back. "I imagine so. Do you want to talk about it?"

With a sniff, Keegan pulled away. "No. Thank you, though. It's not that I don't want to talk as much as I don't know what to say. I came here, hoping to see a friend and get away. Not for this. Maybe I should just go home."

"Do you really plan to let a man steal your vacation? On top of everything else, will you let him have this too?" Micah looked fierce. His expression sparked a fire inside Keegan. He was right. Did

Keegan intend to let Omen show up here and break him?

"I paid a lot of money for this trip."

Micah nodded. "I imagine so."

The spark grew brighter, turning hot. "I was really excited about meeting you and spending time with Detroit."

"You should keep your plans. In fact, come to side stage with me and watch the bands play, even his. Hold your head high and have fun. If I had an ex here, I'd smile so brightly he'd leave here questioning his every decision. I'd send him to bed wondering if I planned to be in someone else's. Get in his line of sight. Make him sorry for showing up."

Keegan found himself nodding along. He should put himself in Omen's path. Let him see Keegan could live without him. He could do this. Omen didn't deserve to know he'd destroyed Keegan.

"Yes. Let's do it."

Micah's adorable smile turned bright. "That's the spirit. Make him sorry."

He would. Omen would regret losing him for the rest of his life if Keegan had any say. After all, it was only fair. Keegan shouldn't be the only one who woke up every day feeling like he was missing a limb. Driver stood nearby, putting away the paints. Keegan couldn't take it. He focused on Micah. "I'll meet up with you in a few."

Micah glanced Driver's way and nodded as if he understood. "Just be there by ten, okay? You don't want Omen to miss you as he comes off stage. Promise me."

Keegan bit back a laugh. Even when Micah tried to be stern, he was adorable. "Cross my heart. I have my VIP badge and I won't miss it."

Micah's bright smile made Keegan's day better. "Good. I'll keep an eye out for you."

He waited until Micah walked away before moving closer to Driver. Keegan twisted the lanyard around his neck to give his hands something to do. He wasn't good at apologizing. "Do you want some help?"

Driver glanced over, looking surprised he wasn't alone. "No. I'm good. Micah has people to clean all this up. I just..." He shrugged. "Didn't have anything else, I guess."

Keegan relieved Driver of the paints, setting them back on the table before linking his arm through Driver's. He tugged him away from the table. "Not true. You have me. Let's go."

The way Driver dragged his feet screamed reluctance. "Um. Where?"

"To find a drink. Listen to some music. Dance. You know, the whole shebang."

"Yeah, I don't do those things."

Keegan shook his head and sighed at Driver's response. "You're so dark and moody. It's okay to tap your foot to some music. No one will judge you for not silently punishing yourself for five minutes."

Driver stopped dragging his feet but kept bitching. "You make a lot of assumptions for someone who doesn't know me."

"Feel free to tell me when I'm wrong," Keegan practically sang, hoping to pull some humor from Driver.

"You're wrong."

"Ha. Prove it." Keegan heard the daring in his voice. He couldn't stop. There was something about Driver. Keegan liked him. He turned, walking backwards before stepping into Driver's path and forcing the man to stop. "Dance. Come on. Show me some moves."

Driver's light blue gaze skirted away. "Um, that's a no for me."

Keegan nodded. "Okay. Smile."

"Have you been drinking?"

A huff escaped Keegan. "See? Dark. Moody. Self-punisher. And, for your information, I don't

45

need to drink to be annoying. I'm a natural. Also, I'm sorry about earlier."

A hint of a smile touched Driver's lips. "You had your reasons."

"I had reasons but no excuse," Keegan said, refusing to have his apology brushed aside. "Cortland is your friend. If you don't want to risk messing that up, then that's totally your decision. I had no business putting in my two cents. Seeing as how I don't have any friends back home, I really didn't have two cents to spare."

"Cortland shot me down."

"Oh." Keegan didn't know what else to say. He hadn't expected that.

With a sigh, Driver draped his arm over Keegan's shoulders and started walking. "So you don't have any friends back home. That's surprising. I mean, you're a pain in the ass, but in a lovable sort of way."

Keegan smiled as he wrapped his arm around Driver's waist and matched his pace. "Yeah. I'm not for everyone."

"You can be for me for the rest of the day. How about that?"

A soft chuckle rumbled from Keegan. "Sounds good. In fact, I'm here for the next two weeks. Maybe we can find something else to do while I'm here."

Driver laughed. Keegan nearly stumbled at the sound. It was damn sexy. "Are you asking me on a date?"

Keegan thought it over. He could do worse than a nice if not a little moody guy like Driver. "Maybe I am."

"I've had worse offers."

Keegan pinched Driver's side and pushed him away. "Never mind. I'll be washing my hair for the next two weeks."

After rubbing the spot Keegan pinched, Driver risked his skin again by draping his arm over Keegan's shoulders once more. His smile didn't abate. "I'd love to go out sometime if you're willing. Still, I feel I should warn you, I'll probably scare the hell out of you. People find me somewhat intense."

Keegan wasn't worried. He already knew they'd only be friends. It was more than obvious neither of them had a heart to spare. Omen would probably always own Keegan's, and—shot down or not—Cortland obviously owned Driver. That didn't mean they couldn't have lunch sometime. Who knew? Maybe one day Keegan could move on.

THE CROWD WAS huge and loud for a charity event. If circumstances had been different, Omen would've been blown away by their excitement. As it was, his gaze wouldn't stop straying to side stage. Several times, he'd caught sight of Keegan dancing, laughing, and openly teasing the man who'd threatened Omen earlier. It was no wonder the man had been so worried about Keegan. It was beyond obvious he'd fallen under Keegan's spell. As much as Omen wanted to be pissed, he couldn't. It was Keegan. He was an irresistible combination of gorgeous, confident, and fun. No one was immune.

Omen waited until he'd dashed back on stage for the final time to launch his new song. As planned, the lights dropped low, and the spotlight landed on him alone. He stepped close to the microphone. "This is an unreleased song. I saved it just for you guys." The crowd roared. Omen waited until they quieted before speaking again. "This one is for Keegan." He took a deep breath. It sounded loud against the mic. He focused on his guitar, found the right strings, and strummed before leaning toward the microphone again. Omen sang the words he wrote the night Keegan left him. "It was late the night we met, yet you let me in. Bet you regret that now." He paused to play a few chords.

"All I wanted was to feel your skin. Bet you regret me now." His nerves settled a hair as he nodded, falling into the music. "It's no surprise to me that I ruined everything. Bet you regret us now." He took a breath and picked up the pace. "I never wanted this. All I crave is your kiss. I could swear I'll change, but you know me too well. All I'm good for is not much. I guarantee I'll make your life hell. Still, I go to sleep each night longing for your touch."

Omen kept singing, losing himself in the words. He poured his soul into the song. Keegan was out there somewhere. This would be everywhere before Omen even left the stage. It didn't matter. Nothing mattered except Keegan and fixing the damage he'd done. Keegan deserved to be publicly claimed, even if he never forgave Omen or took him back. Omen had to set things right. The guitar fell silent as the final words left his lips. Omen didn't lift his gaze to the crowd as he turned away from the mic. His steps faltered as he headed off stage. Keegan was there, waiting side stage. Their gazes met. Omen didn't slow. He passed his guitar to the first semi-familiar face. Before Omen reached his side, Keegan turned and walked away. Omen couldn't breathe. He picked up the pace, going after him. Several people tried stopping him, but Omen pushed his way past them, refusing to lose Keegan in the crowd.

"Keegan, please? Hold up and talk to me."

At his plea, Keegan came to an abrupt halt and spun. He closed the distance between them so fast, Omen expected to get hit. Instead, Keegan got in his face. "No. I don't want to talk. Haven't you noticed me walking away when you show up? It's because there's nothing to say. All you have is words, Omen, and you don't mean half of what you say. I stayed and listened to your song because Micah made me. But no, I have no time for you. Yes, that song was sweet, but I know *you*." Keegan put such an emphasis of distaste on that final word, Omen almost took a step back. "If I agree to go somewhere and talk," Keegan said, using air quotes, "we'll fuck, and that's all it'll be to you. Tomorrow will come, and someone will reach out to you, asking for a statement on your new song dedicated to Keegan. I can already hear you saying I'm just a friend." Keegan's voice broke and shattered Omen's heart. When Keegan spoke again, his voice came out in a whisper, as if he couldn't talk louder without crying. "I am not your friend. Friends don't hurt."

Omen couldn't back down. This was the first time Keegan looked his way since catching him kissing Detroit. Omen had to speak now before Keegan got away. "You're right. We're not friends. I love you. If you never kiss me again, then we'll never be anything at all, because I can't be your friend. But when it comes to what I'll tell people, you're wrong. I did an interview with *Today's Metal* before tonight's show, during which I told them I planned to debut a new song tonight. About you. Us." Keegan looked frozen. Omen kept talking. "I told them how we met. Why I lost you. I told them everything."

"What?" The question was a harsh whisper that could've been pain, rage, or anything in between.

While hoping for the best, Omen nodded. "You're so damn strong and brave. I've always wished I could be like you. You deserve for me to be like you."

"Why are you doing this to me? There are millions of other people you could break. Why me?"

"I have an SUV waiting to take me to the hotel. Come with me. Please? I miss your voice. I'll answer anything you want to know."

Keegan visibly took a breath. "I don't think that's a good idea."

"Do I need to get on my knees and beg?" Omen asked, shuffling closer. "You know I'll do it. I'll make a huge scene."

Even though he looked away, Keegan wasn't fast enough to hide his smile. When he met Omen's stare again, he looked resigned. "Twenty minutes."

Omen did a little hop, not bothering to hide his triumph. "Can my twenty minutes start after I take a shower? I'm sweaty and gross."

An exasperated-sounding huff escaped Keegan. "I guess, but only because I don't want to smell you."

After clasping his hands behind his back to keep from touching Keegan, Omen fell into step beside the man. "You used to love my sweat."

"Only the sweat I caused." Keegan's grumbled words sent a wave of lust washing over Omen. He missed this. His body longed for the nights Keegan spent beneath him. They fit together perfectly. Fuck, they just belonged together.

Keegan tucked a strand of unruly dark hair behind his ear and glanced Omen's way. Omen's gut tightened. He loved and missed every tiny thing about Keegan. "So, um, where are you staying?"

Omen opened the back door to the SUV and waved Keegan inside. "The Luna." He drew Keegan's scent into his lungs. Damn, he wanted to touch him. The longing ate at his brain, making him crazy.

"Me too," Keegan said as he buckled in. He

clutched his bag to his chest, looking nervous. "I hoped to see one of Detroit's fights while I'm here."

The bag Keegan held captured Omen's attention. It looked like a small backpack. Keegan never went anywhere without it. He was diabetic. The bag was his emergency kit, filled with snacks and insulin. It was such a stupid thing to stab him through the heart, but he knew what was inside. That seemed intimate—like something only someone in love would know. Omen had to clear his throat to speak. "It seems like Detroit and you have grown close."

Keegan clutched the bag tighter—like a lifeline. Omen wished he could reach over and soothe Keegan's fears with his touch. "I suppose. You know I don't have many friends."

That was true. People didn't understand Keegan. He didn't fit anyone's ideals in any group. Keegan wasn't a transgender person. He wore makeup because he liked it. A lot of his clothes were made for women but weren't necessarily girlie. They looked perfect on him. He was covered in tattoos. Keegan was unique. He couldn't be put in a box. Unfortunately, he lived in a world that expected a category for everyone. Since he didn't fit anywhere, most people didn't accept him. Omen was glad

Detroit had reached out to Keegan. He didn't like the thought of Keegan being alone. There was a sting of jealousy too, but only because Omen was a bad person. Detroit was married and happy. It was funny the things that didn't matter to the heart. Omen wanted Keegan all to himself.

"I'm in the penthouse," Omen said, steering things into safer waters.

Keegan nodded. "That makes sense. Otherwise, you'd be a security nightmare."

He wasn't surprised Keegan didn't offer his room number. Keegan had agreed to twenty minutes. That was all Omen would get.

While twisting his bag's straps, Keegan cleared his throat. "Have you seen Detroit fight before? This Friday will be my first time. I'm not sure what to expect."

Omen accepted the subject change. As much as he might want to, he couldn't force things. "Once. In Vegas. Honestly, it's pretty brutal."

Keegan nodded. "I worried it might be. Detroit seems solid—like he could take some punishment."

It was too hard. Omen couldn't keep talking about other things. "I'm sorry." The words were out there before Omen could change his mind. "For everything I've ever done." Omen had to say it all.

Now, before it was too late. "You scare me like no one I've ever met. Not because meeting you made me question everything about myself, but because you're the first person who made me want to settle down. You're also the last for me. I don't want anyone else but you."

The way Keegan's expression remained closed didn't instill confidence in Omen. "Your mouth says one thing, but the last time I saw you, you were kissing Detroit. I'm at a loss with you. How many chances do you think you deserve? I'm a person with feelings, you know? I get that you think the world revolves around you, and you're used to having everything you want, but what about me? Do I factor at all?"

"I know. I hear you." In truth, Omen didn't know how to respond without digging his hole deeper. "You've always known who you are. I'm trying."

A loud and obnoxious-sounding laugh escaped Keegan. "You think I don't confuse myself sometimes? Do you honestly think my life is easy?"

Omen tried not to panic. This wasn't going well. There was so much hunger in his gut when Keegan was around, but he wasn't allowed to touch the man he loved. It was hell. "I know it's not. People don't see you the way I do. I know you deal with a lot of bullshit all the time just to be true to yourself. Before you walked away from us, I thought facing the questions about us would be too hard. Then, you were gone, and I realized that losing you was the worst and hardest thing I've ever dealt with. Telling people about us turned out to be no problem at all." Keegan was there, listening, and Omen couldn't stop pouring his heart out while he had the chance. "I know it'll take work to get back to the way we were, but I'm willing to do anything you need me to do to prove myself."

Exasperation etched Keegan's features. "I don't want to go back to the way we were. You kept me a secret, remember? No. I don't want the old us."

Omen scrubbed his fingers through his hair, ready to tear it out at the roots. "You're not hearing me. I love you. This is a real thing," he said, motioning between them. "Not only do I not want a secret relationship, I want the whole world to know you're mine. That you're off the shelf. You come home to me."

Keegan looked away. "We're here. Take your shower. You'll be on the clock soon."

With an aggravated growl, Omen climbed from the vehicle. People took out their phones as he passed, the way they always did, trying to snap pictures of him before he disappeared. Keegan tried walking behind him. Omen kept slowing, refusing to let him be anywhere but at Omen's side. Twice he reached for Keegan's hand, but Keegan found ways to dodge him. Irritation owned him. He didn't know how to fix things if Keegan wouldn't let him. Damn, he was more than willing to let people snap pictures of them together, holding hands. Keegan wasn't having it. The guy was maddening. Keegan didn't want to be kept a secret. He wouldn't let Omen publicly claim him. Omen wanted to scream.

When they made it to his room, Omen grabbed Keegan a bottle of water and then ran for the shower. He didn't put it past Keegan to bail the second Omen wasn't around to stop him from leaving. It was a record time shower. He barely let the water get hot. Nothing mattered like getting back to Keegan. In fact, he didn't bother dressing. After barely passing the towel through his dripping hair, Omen wrapped the material around his waist and headed back out to Keegan. He was more than a little surprised to find him still sitting on the couch where he'd left him.

Omen's steps slowed while he eyed Keegan. He sat, holding his bag with his water perched on top. His gaze scanned the room, taking in the suite's luxury. The place was damn nice for a hotel room with its full kitchen, living room, and three bedrooms. From what Omen gathered, the owner of the Luna always stayed in this room when conducting business. Detroit had secured it for Omen as part of Detroit donating his time for Micah's charity. Still, the place had nothing on Keegan. He was all Omen cared to see. His messy dark hair and dark blue eyes always haunted Omen's dreams. The way the two piercings in Keegan's bottom lip felt when they kissed or sliding down Omen's cock; that was something Omen couldn't shake. He'd never been the type to get obsessed with anything that wasn't music related. His career was everything. Music lived in his veins and filled his head. Then, he'd locked himself inside Keegan's store, looking for refuge. He'd turned and set eyes on Keegan. Time had stopped. His mind had fallen silent. Looking at Keegan now, nothing had changed. Omen's knees were still weak. The hands on the clock were meaningless. He was raw emotion with no words.

Keegan's head turned. His gaze swept Omen's body. "You forgot your clothes." The flush on his cheeks and the lust in his voice belied Keegan's words.

"You said I have twenty minutes starting after

58

my shower. I didn't want to cut into my time with dressing." Omen crossed the room. Keegan tilted his chin up, holding Omen's stare as he came to stand over him. He didn't think. Omen simply relieved Keegan of his bag and water, setting them aside, before hauling Keegan to his feet.

"If I only have twenty minutes, I don't want to waste it with words you won't believe." He dipped his head and captured Keegan's lips, risking a knee to his very unprotected nuts. For a moment, Keegan stood stiffly beneath his kiss. His fingertips skimmed Omen's sides. The move startled Omen so much his body jerked. Keegan shuffled closer. His caress transformed into a hold. Their bodies met. Omen went hard. His towel wasn't nearly enough protection.

"I've missed you so much. All I think about is you," Omen said as he changed angles. His hands filled with Keegan's ass as he hauled the man against him, ensuring his erection wasn't missed.

Keegan fought every bit as hard to get closer to Omen. The towel fell away. Keegan's fingers encircled Omen's erection. The breath left Omen's lungs. He tore at Keegan's clothes, pulling off the man's shirt before quickly reclaiming Keegan's mouth. When he found the button of Keegan's pants,

Omen couldn't resist pulling away again. He had to see.

"Please be lace. Please be lace," Omen chanted as he unzipped Keegan's pants. His hand dove inside. "Yes." A wave of desire consumed him. He loved the way Keegan's cock felt with lace panties cupping him. He stared down the line of Keegan's body, mouth watering as he peeled Keegan's pants down his thighs. "Please say it's also a thong." He spun Keegan in his arms. "Goddamn. So sexy." The words came out sounding breathless, even to his ears. "It's like you always dress just for me."

"I dress for me, but you're always in the back of my mind."

Keegan's confession stole a piece of Omen. Omen wasn't alone in his feelings. Keegan hadn't fully given up on them. There was hope. The knowledge had Omen kissing his way down Keegan's spine. His cock jerked as he dragged the lace down Keegan's hips. A loud moan reverberated from the walls as Omen's teeth sank into Keegan's ass cheek. Sometimes, Omen couldn't get close enough to Keegan to soothe his heart. Omen took his time stripping Keegan bare. He kissed every place he could reach before coming back to his feet. As much as he wanted to attack Keegan, falling on him with every bit of the insanity in his heart, Omen equally wanted to savor their time together. He hadn't touched Keegan in months. His heart needed him to go slow.

───────

OMEN WENT from ripping Keegan's clothes away to moving painfully slow. Keegan fought the urge to scream. For months, he'd been empty. Once they were both nude, Omen sat on the couch. He tried pulling Keegan into his lap. Keegan wasn't having it. He bent and licked Omen's crown. His eyes fell closed as Omen's delicious flavor washed over his taste buds. Keegan could still remember the first time he'd done this to Omen.

He lifted his gaze as he kissed a path down Omen's body. Omen looked torn between turned on and embarrassed. His cheeks were flushed, but a bit too much—like a blush.

"Why are you embarrassed, baby?"

Omen covered his eyes for a moment. His blush deepened. "This is my first time like this. With a man, I mean. If I was a woman, you'd feel out of your element too."

"Not true," Keegan said, licking Omen's erection

and pulling a low moan from Omen. "I've eaten pussy." He savored Omen's shock as he pushed the man's thighs wider and moved lower. "It was awesome. I loved the way they squirmed as I licked their clits." He tongued the spot between Omen's balls and asshole. Omen scratched at the sheets. Keegan bit back a smile even as his cock leaked onto the sheets beneath him. "They always moaned as I did things no straight man would." Keegan punctuated his claim by tonguing Omen's asshole, coating him with saliva. He gripped Omen's cock, pumping. Keegan knew he was about to truly push Omen out of his comfort zone. He would either stay or go, but Keegan needed to know now. "I'll do things for you too. Make you moan." That was all the warning Keegan gave before he shifted upward and swallowed Omen's cock while pushing two fingers inside him. Keegan curled his fingers, massaging the spot that he knew would drive Omen insane. He sucked in time with his fingers. His scalp stung as Omen pulled him closer. Omen's body was hard and tight as he cursed and moaned. Keegan knew how to please him. Make him addicted.

Nothing had changed, except now Omen knew what Keegan could do for him. His hungry stare said he couldn't wait as Keegan slipped to his knees between Omen's and pushed the man's thighs farther apart. He massaged the spot between Omen's balls and asshole.

"Have you touched yourself the way I touch you?"

"So many times since you've been gone," Omen admitted in a harsh-sounding whisper. "It never felt the same."

Keegan's thumb moved lower, barely skimming the ring of Omen's hole. Omen's breathing turned ragged. Keegan's hunger grew. "Did you whisper my name while you fingered yourself?"

"Every time."

At Omen's admission, Keegan hauled the man closer until his ass hung over the edge of the couch. He forced Omen's knees wider. Keegan held Omen's stare as he leaned in. He'd never seen Omen look needier. His eyes fell closed as he shamelessly tongued Omen's asshole, circling and teasing. Omen scratched at the couch and tugged at Keegan's hair, openly seeking purchase as he cried for more.

Reaching between his legs, Keegan squeezed his cock, trying to relieve the pressure growing inside him. Omen wasn't the only one being tortured. He loved sucking and licking, giving pleasure. The sounds Omen made drove him insane. Keegan took Omen down his throat.

"I don't want to come like this," Omen said, sounding needy. "Come here."

Keegan moved to his feet. Omen pulled him into his lap. Keegan's spine and bare ass molded to Omen's overheated body. Omen's dick stood between Keegan's legs, caressing Keegan's balls. Keegan reached down and massaged Omen's cock, tugging him tighter against his body. He writhed in Omen's arms, needing more.

"Get a condom from your bag. I know there's one in there."

Keegan grabbed his bag from where it sat on the couch beside them. He dug inside, finding a condom and a travel-sized tube of lube that went everywhere with him. Between the two of them and several kisses and open strokes, they got Omen suited up. Oily lube was everywhere. He didn't care. Keegan needed Omen inside him.

Keegan balanced his weight on his heels and lifted enough for Omen to position his cock. He lowered himself onto Omen's erection. Omen's dick stretched him and filled him. Keegan fought the urge to move, riding Omen fast and taking his pleasure. Instead, he molded against Omen, letting his man pump Keegan's cock as he slowly pumped inside Keegan's ass. Omen licked and sucked at Keegan's ear. He whispered words of love that barely penetrated Keegan's lust-fogged brain. Sweat coated their skin. Neither of them sped things along. Keegan's body was on fire. It begged for relief. Keegan's brain pleaded for the moment to never end. He wasn't ready to go back to being alone. To whispering Omen's name into the empty darkness. It was hell to love someone he would never really own.

Omen's hold tightened on Keegan's dick. He pumped faster, as if jacking his own cock. Keegan could tell by the way Omen's body tensed beneath him, he was getting close. He closed his eyes and let the pleasure wash over him. The sensation of Omen's palm on his dick was amazing. His body drew up tighter with each stroke. Keegan's hips moved, seeking more until he openly fucked Omen's hand.

With his head tilted back on Omen's shoulder, Keegan stared at the ceiling, seeing nothing and gasping for air. Omen was in control. The spring coiled inside him snapped. Keegan's body shook as an orgasm slammed into him. Jets of cum shot from his dick, coating his skin. Omen's teeth sank into Keegan's shoulder as he pushed as deep as he could go. Muffled cries flowed from Omen, bringing tears to Keegan's eyes. He didn't understand how something could feel so good and right and still hurt so damn bad. That was what it was like loving Omen —painful perfection.

"Come to bed with me," Omen whispered against his ear, sounding breathless. "Let me hold you and fall asleep with your head on my chest. I miss that. I miss you."

Keegan couldn't deny him. It wasn't even about Omen's claims of love or missing him. It was him. Inside, where no one could see, Keegan was a slave to Omen. That was why he stayed away, changed his number, and avoided him at all costs. He knew himself. Omen owned him.

He gave Omen his wish. His heart squeezed, and his lungs wouldn't expand. Every second he spent in Omen's arms was torment. Keegan understood too well what it was like not to have him. Watching Omen sleep was like living in his own personal hell. The absolute knowledge that Keegan had allowed Omen to use him again sat heavy on his chest. Keegan didn't know how he knew. He just did. There was something eating at the back of his mind. Something felt wrong. Keegan knew nothing good would come of this night. He felt the knowledge growing inside him, getting bigger with each passing second. Being near Omen always struck him dumb. He wasn't immune to Omen's star status. Power in any form was sexy as fuck and irresistible. Omen made people want to touch him. Be near him. Keegan was no different or better. All it ever took was fifteen minutes in Omen's company, at most, and Keegan was shimmying off his clothes.

Omen claimed he'd told the world about them. Did that mean people were already spreading the word? He'd never believed they would be a real couple. Keegan had a hard time swallowing it now too. His mind got the better of him. After slipping from the bed, Keegan found his phone. He searched Omen's name. A gazillion results came back. They were all music related as far as Keegan could tell. He added "gay" to the end of Omen's name. Articles and pictures of Omen and Detroit in Vegas came back. Nothing about Keegan. Keegan paced. He chewed his bottom lip while the feeling in his gut grew. Keegan stopped. Each breath came faster and harder as he stared at his phone. His heartbeat pounded in his ears. It was possible the article hadn't released yet, but Keegan doubted they'd sit on such a juicy story. He searched the name of the magazine. Zero results.

Keegan's eyes fell closed. His throat swelled, and his eyes itched with unshed tears. Another lie. He'd fallen for another goddamn pretty tale. Fuck. He'd wanted to believe. His heart had longed for Omen's words to be true. For a moment, Keegan stood clutching his phone and lost in the pain. He could wake Omen—make a scene. Keegan could scream and stamp his feet. Why bother? He'd done this to himself. Each and every fucking time Omen breezed into his life, Keegan had done this to himself.

Without glancing Omen's way, Keegan went in search of all his things. He dressed in silence. His emotions were on lockdown. This was the last time he'd be weak. Omen had finally taught him the lesson Keegan needed. He'd really thought he'd learned when he'd caught Omen kissing Detroit, but no. Detroit had chipped his armor by befriending Keegan. But now, there were no more excuses. Omen had broken him for the last time. He was done.

FOUR

KEEGAN STARED THROUGH THE PEEPHOLE AT Detroit as the man banged on his hotel room door. A tiny part of him considered not answering. He'd never been able to hold a grudge. It was a little aggravating, actually. He'd always been the type to get over things quickly. Keegan was too empathetic. He usually saw all sides. Detroit cared about him. He thought he understood what Keegan needed, and he'd tried to make it happen. That was sweet. Ugh. Keegan opened the door.

"I'm sorry."

At Detroit's immediate apology, Keegan's shoulders fell. He opened the door wider. "Come in." Even Keegan heard the petulance in his tone.

Detroit stepped inside the room and closed the

door behind him. Keegan's annoyance ratcheted up another notch as he got a good look at the man. The dark circles beneath his eyes and the way his hair stood on end said he hadn't slept at all, and he was still hot. No doubt Keegan looked every bit as shitty as he felt. Yet here Detroit was—tight t-shirt and jeans that protested his muscular thighs. Life wasn't fair.

"While talking things over with Payne last night, I realized some things."

Keegan dropped onto the bed and stared at Detroit in agitated expectance. "Such as?"

"You haven't known me long," Detroit answered, as if it explained everything.

"Okay." Really. That was all Keegan had. His head hurt too badly to try for more.

Without invitation, Detroit climbed into Keegan's bed. He sat so close their thighs touched. Up close, he was even hotter. Keegan thought he hated him a little. "You only know the me that I've shown you, because it was nice to have a friend who's only known me for as long as I've been happy," Detroit said, still not making sense. Thankfully, he didn't make Keegan dig for clarification. "See, you said yesterday that I don't understand because no one has ever been ashamed of me. You're wrong.

Everyone has always been ashamed of me, including me." He had Keegan's attention. "I didn't tell you I'm married to Micah's dad, because I was his secret for a long time. It was nice being friends with someone who didn't know I fell in love with my best friend's dad and lied nonstop to everyone. I liked having a friend who didn't know how that fucked me up. Someone who didn't know how it almost killed me." He set his arm on Keegan's thigh, forearm up, revealing angry-looking scars Keegan hadn't noticed before now. Keegan traced the ragged edges with his fingertip. He had no words. Detroit covered Keegan's hand with his. "It's not been long enough yet for me to forget what it was like to be alone, drowning, and searching for any escape. I shouldn't have sprung Omen on you. I just don't want you to be alone, unhappy, and searching for any escape. Not if I can help."

Keegan's eyes burned. He kept his gaze locked on their joined hands so Detroit wouldn't see the tears in his eyes. Not once had he thought of suicide, but he couldn't deny he was tired. It had only been hours since he'd walked away from Omen again and he was just so damn exhausted. Plus, it broke his heart knowing Detroit had ever been in that much pain. "I know you thought you were helping."

"I was wrong," Detroit said, squeezing his hand. "So we'll do whatever you want to do. I swear I won't interfere again. If you want to change hotels, I'll pay for you to stay elsewhere. Or, if you're interested, I have a good friend who owns a huge house right on the ocean. You'd have a private beach at your disposal and you'd likely never see anyone else who lives there. That's how big the place is. I've already asked if I could invite you. Since Zander knows I'm a huge fuck up, not only was he not surprised, he was happy to help. That way, there's no chance you'll encounter Omen again while you're here."

Keegan tried swiping at his eyes on the sly. "Who is Zander?"

"He owns the hotel you're sitting in."

A watery laugh escaped Keegan. "Of course he does. Is there anyone you don't know?"

"Lots of people. Fair warning, though. For full disclosure's sake. If you choose to stay at Zander's, just know you'd be a guest of the mob."

Laughter tore from Keegan's throat. He didn't doubt for a moment Detroit was telling the truth, but it still struck him as hilarious. "I'll stay with him." Why the hell not? His life had been an insane ride so far. He might as well get some mafia connections.

AFTER DRAGGING his chair to the window, Omen kicked back and stared at the ocean. He could leave. In fact, he needed to get back to his tour. Instead, he chose to stay one more night in the bed he'd shared with Keegan. He'd tried. No one could say he hadn't. The interview he'd done with *Today's Metal* had gone live on the web hours earlier. For the rest of his life, he'd know he'd done right by Keegan, even though they were over. He wouldn't chase him again.

Detroit had tried calling several times. Omen let it go to voicemail. He didn't want to talk. There was nothing left to say. All he wanted was to sit still and let the memories overtake him.

Omen's dick ached. He was so hard and ready. With Keegan crowded against the wall of the dark alley, it would be so easy to sneak in a quick fuck. He couldn't do it. Not only did Omen need to get back inside the recording studio, it was past time for Keegan to get home if he wanted to open his shop in the morning. But, damn, it had been a long night without touching his man.

"You're too much temptation. I'm pretty sure you've ruined me for anyone else."

"Awww," Keegan cooed against his lips, trying to pull Omen back in for more.

Omen leaned away while holding Keegan's face. He needed to see Keegan's sexy lips swollen from kissing him. "I'm being serious."

"I know you a—"

"I love you," Omen said, cutting Keegan off.

Keegan licked his lips, looking nervous. "You don't have to say that."

"It's true. Things aren't ideal, I know, but I love you. I'm in love with you. You're all I think about."

The way Keegan visibly melted had Omen ready to throw the man over his shoulder and run away for good. "I love you too."

A metal door opened and closed in the distance. Omen dropped his hands and looked around but didn't see anyone. He went back to staring at Keegan. "You have no idea how much I wish I didn't have to get back to work."

"I know," Keegan said, waving off his claim. "The guys are waiting on you and you've been out here for a while."

Omen reclaimed Keegan's mouth, kissing away all the excuses. No one had ever stolen him like this. Made him want them over music. Still, he had to go.

"I love you," he whispered one more time as he pulled away.

"Love you too," Keegan whispered back. He stepped around Omen and inside his car, setting Omen free.

"I'll call you tomorrow." Omen closed Keegan's door on the promise and headed back inside. Cabot leaned against the wall right inside the door. His gaze moved over Omen's face, and Omen knew. Cabot had seen. His gut twisted with nerves. The last thing he wanted was to drive a wedge between his band members and himself. Omen could tell by the drummer's expression that he didn't approve.

"You want to tell me what's really going on with Keegan?"

Omen stepped around him. They needed to get back to recording. "I imagine whatever you think is going on is what's going on."

"It's not that I'm judging."

"Good," Omen said, keeping up the pace as he headed for the booth.

"But whatever happens to your reputation, happens to this whole band."

"But you're not judging," Omen said with a snort.

"I'm not." Cabot pulled Omen to a stop before he could get away. "I'm not," he repeated when he had

Omen's full attention. "Just don't lose sight of the big picture, okay? We're about to start a multi-million-dollar tour."

Omen got it. He wasn't in the position to choose Keegan over everything else right now. "Don't worry. It's fine. Keegan knows all this and is cool with everything. He likes y'all. He wants us to go out there and crush it."

Cabot nodded. The relief written in his expression tightened Omen's throat. Every day it got a little harder. People were depending on him. That was a hell of thing while he was drowning.

Nothing had changed except everything. Keegan no longer cared what anyone thought. But he was still drowning. Every day. Nonstop. Even though he'd tried and lost, Omen wouldn't trade a single minute. No matter how much it hurt, whether he ever caught his breath, Omen remembered moments he'd never shared with anyone else.

No matter how many people Omen played for or how many songs he'd written, Omen was always nervous the first time he sang a new song. Sharing his songs was like exposing a piece of his soul, opening it up for ridicule. He wasn't the type to write bullshit. Every song he'd written was true to life. Keegan didn't know it, but lately, each new song was for him.

The way Keegan watched him as he sang made it hard for Omen to stay on tempo. Sitting cross-legged on the floor, with his guitar balanced on his knee, Omen switched his gaze to his hands when Keegan's stare became too intense.

"I'm sorry," Keegan said, interrupting him. "I'm having a hard time hearing the words now."

Omen forced his chin up.

Keegan scooted closer. A line appeared between his eyes, and he leaned even closer. "I'm sorry," Keegan repeated. "Let's try this." Without warning, Keegan plucked the guitar from Omen's hold. He set it aside and straddled Omen's lap. "There we go. Now, sing."

Omen's palms automatically swept up Keegan's back. He pulled him closer. Hunger and love built inside him. He pressed his lips to Keegan's ear and sang. Keegan smelled like cotton candy and hope. He was warm, and Omen felt full. In that moment, he was home. Wherever Keegan was, Omen was home.

Yeah, Omen had his memories. They were pretty damn amazing.

FIVE

After a five-hour unexpected layover, Keegan didn't make it home until eleven p.m. He stumbled through his dark apartment, dragging suitcases behind him and cursing his aching legs. Staying with Zander and his husband Maverick turned out to be the best decision Keegan had ever made. The pair had made him feel beyond welcome before leaving him alone to do this own thing. Topping things off, they'd given Keegan carte blanche to their personal driver, ensuring he got to see as much of the city as he liked while in town. He'd spent time with Driver, finding a new friend. Detroit had kept him company as much as possible. Now his head swam with exhaustion. Still, he started a load of laundry and went through his mail. The flashing red numbers on his answering machine caught his eye. There were over fifty messages. He hadn't known his machine held that many. Not to mention, no one ever called him. The only reason he kept a landline was for store business and his security alarm. He pressed play. Thirty seconds in, his heart stopped beating correctly. He couldn't catch his breath.

"This is Allen Wright with *Today's Metal*. I'd hoped to get a quote from you to add to an article I'm writing about Omen Birch." Keegan's heart beat so loudly inside his ears it drowned out the man's next words. Each message was more of the same. People wanting quotes. Unknown voices and names, wanting to know if the rumors were true. Was he, in fact, dating Omen Birch?

Keegan blindly felt for a chair. He found one at the kitchen table. His hands shook as he sat, staring at nothing. Omen had been telling the truth. He'd been telling the truth and Keegan had left. Sneaked away in the middle of the night. Holy shit. What had he done? Shock, happiness, and fear pulled him in different directions. He should call Omen. Beg for forgiveness. It was the middle of the night. Omen probably wouldn't answer. Keegan covered his mouth. His eyes burned. A tear slid down his cheek.

Omen had really done it. He'd told the world about Keegan. What if he'd fucked up any chance of being together?

Keegan shot to his feet and scrambled for his phone. He had to try.

The phone shook in his hands as he searched for Omen's number. He stabbed at the man's name, trying to get the phone to dial. His motions were so frantic, his touchscreen didn't want to register his touch. Finally, ringing filled the air. It rang once and went straight to voicemail—like Omen's phone was turned off. Keegan had to stop himself from chucking the device across the room in his aggravation.

Instead, his mind raced, searching for another way to be closer to Omen. He searched the web, looking for his tour schedule. His mind screeched to a halt and his breathing evened out. Omen was in Baton Rouge tonight. The final concert of his tour. No doubt it had already ended. His man was only two hours away. That meant Omen was—most likely —coming home tomorrow.

Keegan hugged the phone to his chest and stared at nothing. He could wait. Tomorrow was soon enough. Once he closed up shop tomorrow night, he'd go after him. No phone calls. He'd show up and beg in person. If Keegan had messed up and Omen never wanted to see him again, Omen would have to say that to Keegan's face. One thought kept floating through his mind without ceasing. Please God. Don't let it be too late.

———

BATON ROUGE WAS IT. The final stop on a long-ass tour that had wiped him mentally and physically. Soon, he'd be home. Minutes from Keegan. One more night. That was all. Sweat rolled down Omen's chest. His shirt plastered to his wet back. The heat from the stage lights felt ten times hotter than usual. A sharp pain stabbed him in the neck and his head felt stuffed with cotton. He had a bad feeling he'd caught a bug somewhere in the past day or so. He'd tried eating earlier, but nothing tasted good or right. Omen couldn't decide if he was sick or depressed. He'd never felt like this before. Everything was just... off.

The crowd chanted his name, calling for an encore. He'd do one more song. Keegan's song, and then he was done for the night. Maybe Omen would skip the hotel and head for home. He could be back in New Orleans by one in the morning. Hell, maybe he'd swing by Keegan's and make sure the man made it safely home from California. Or maybe he'd beg Detroit for Keegan's new number one more time. Who knew? There was a slight chance Detroit might give in this time.

Omen headed back on stage, guitar in hand. For some reason, his legs felt heavier than unusual. His left side tingled like fire ants crawled on his skin. He lost his grip, and the instrument slipped from his numb fingers. Cabot ran toward him. Omen blinked, trying to cling to reality. People surrounded him, talking, but he heard nothing. Then, there was nothing.

KEEGAN SAILED through his usual morning routine. This wasn't a huge time of year for balls or masquerades once Mardi Gras passed, so Keegan didn't do a ton of business. Sometimes, he would get wedding parties looking for something unique for upcoming summer weddings. Mostly, he only got the occasional curious tourist. Since he didn't expect to get hit with a crowd, Keegan did as he pleased. He turned on the radio, blasting music through the building. He smiled as the metal music pounded at his ears. The sun shone bright through the large windows, filling the place with light and warmth. For the first time in months, hope and peace overtook Keegan. The knowledge that he would see Omen later made everything feel lighter. He caught himself shaking his ass to the music. Keegan picked up the pace, laughing as he danced along with the beat and counted his register for the day. Sometimes, being alone was choking. Other times, like now, it was freeing. No one could see him enjoying the moment. The fast-paced song died away and the usual radio personality took over, stuffing Keegan's head with the day's news. Keegan froze when he heard Omen's name.

"Omen Birch, front man for Slight Bastards, collapsed overnight while onstage at Trinity arena. Sources close to the thirty-nine-year-old's family say the man known for his unique metal style suffered a stroke during his performance. Publicist River Howard says Birch is listed in stable condition at Hightower Medical."

Keegan's heart stopped before racing back up again. Luckily, the store was still empty. He ran to the door and flipped the sign to closed before anyone came inside. Hightower was outside Baton Rouge. If he left now, he could be there in under two hours. He didn't think. The idea he might not be welcome never crossed his mind. Nothing mattered except getting to Omen. It wasn't until he was rushing inside the hospital that he considered he might get turned away at the door. Keegan followed a nurse's direction to the stroke floor. He spotted Omen's publicist first. Even though he'd never met River, Keegan had seen the man on TV on several occasions. To his surprise, River headed his way the second he caught sight of Keegan.

"Keegan, right?"

Keegan nodded. The dark-haired man held a hand out for him to shake. "I'm River, Omen's publicist. He's this way," River said, taking Keegan's arm and heading down the hall.

"I wasn't sure if I'd be welcome." Nervousness always used Keegan's mouth without his permission. "It's not like I'm family."

River flashed him an understanding smile. "That's not important. Omen decides who comes and goes. He's been asking about you, but I didn't know how to reach you. The number listed in his phone has been reassigned."

"Yeah. I had it changed last month." There was no need to add he'd changed it so Omen couldn't reach him. "How is Omen?"

"Stable. There's some short-term memory loss

and slight paralysis. You'll see. In here," he added, knocking once before leading Keegan inside.

Omen's gaze slid his way. He blinked, as if he wasn't sure Keegan was real. "Still just like a sunset." Keegan's throat tightened at the words. Omen's gaze moved past Keegan. "Thank you, River. I don't want anyone else to visit."

For a moment, Keegan wondered if he was being thrown out, but River nodded Keegan's way and closed them inside.

"You shouldn't be accepting *any* visitors." The hate-filled words pulled Keegan's gaze away from Omen, finding Omen's mom, Nancy, seated nearby. He hadn't realized they weren't alone. His eyes itched to stay locked on Omen.

"I can go if you're too tired for me."

Omen shook his head. "I've had everyone trying to find you. Things went downhill fast last night. I worried I'd wake up this morning and wouldn't remember all the things I need to say. Stay."

With a nod, Keegan headed for an empty chair next to Omen's bed. He set his bag on the floor between his feet. With nothing left to distract him, Keegan focused on Omen. "What happened? I mean, I know you had a stroke, but you're so young."

"He spends too much time partying," Nancy said before Omen could.

Keegan ignored her. He held Omen's stare, waiting for the real answer.

"They're still doing tests, but I was on stage, and I don't know. Everything in my head felt strange, then my tongue didn't want to work. I thought I was fine and then people were looking at me and asking me weird questions. My left eye wouldn't cooperate. Luckily, I got here fast. They were able to break up the clot. Hopefully, the paralysis and memory loss are only temporary. Either way, it looks like I'm done working for a while."

Keegan twisted the strap on his bag, needing something to do with his hands. "As soon as I turned the radio on in the shop this morning, I heard the news. I closed up the place and got here as soon as I could. You scared me."

"I scared myself."

A knock landed on the door before Keegan could respond. A doctor sailed in, smiling. He was elderly and looked friendly. His hair stood in every direction, as if he hadn't brushed it in days.

"How are you doing this morning, Mr. Birch?"

"Much better."

"Has the nurse been in to go through your memory tests?"

Omen nodded. "About an hour ago."

"How did it go?"

"Better than last night but not perfect. I'm still having trouble with numbers."

The doctor nodded. "It's to be expected that you'll have some problems. It'll get better. The biggest key is rest and no stress. I cannot press that last one enough. Just relax. Keep your blood pressure down."

"My heart is here now," Omen said, motioning toward Keegan. "I'll be fine."

Keegan kept his face blank and hung on every word. Omen had never spoken about him like this in front of people. He didn't know how to react. Keegan couldn't ask the questions he wanted. All he could do was stay and ensure Omen continued existing. Keegan needed him to be somewhere alive, even if they were never together again.

HE DIDN'T FEEL good or right, but having Keegan there lifted his spirits like nothing else could. Omen still couldn't believe he came. Love and fear choked

Omen. He could've died. If he'd passed last night, he never would've gotten to tell Keegan all the things he needed to say. He wouldn't have been able to do everything in his power to make things right. To prove his love.

His mom stood the moment the doctor left them alone. "You heard the doctor. It's time for you to rest."

He was tired, but he had a bad feeling about his mom's expression. She wasn't happy about Keegan. It didn't seem to matter he'd warned her. They'd already talked about this. "I just woke up."

"But surely you don't need all your *friends* sitting around your room while you're trying to heal." The way she said "friends" made her distaste clear, especially since Keegan was the only one there.

Omen glanced Keegan's way. His head was bowed. The way his shoulders stayed squared proved he'd braced for anything. Maybe now wasn't the time, yet it was. "Mom, you know damn well Keegan is more than a friend. Stop lying to yourself to make things easier. I need him here."

She drew herself up to her full five-two status, looking ready for battle. "You're just confused right now. I'll pray for you to get well soon and leave people like this behind. Until then, I'm your mother and I'll care for you. He should go."

"Stop," Omen said, losing his temper. He motioned Keegan's way. "That's a real person sitting there, Mom. Listen to yourself. How can you pretend you're the better person while you berate someone who does nothing but love me? Pray for yourself. It sounds like you need it."

Keegan stood. "It's okay. I'll go."

Panic shot through Omen. He couldn't chase Keegan in his current state, and if Keegan left, Omen might not ever see him again. "No. I don't want you to go."

Keegan took his hand. His sweet smile and the way he held Omen's stare said he gave no fucks about Omen's mom, but Omen knew better. "Listen, baby, you just had a stroke. Now you're getting upset and letting your blood pressure get high. It doesn't matter who's at fault. My being here is obviously an issue. You can't die. It would kill me. I need to go so you can rest."

Omen tightened his hold, refusing to let Keegan go. His frustration rose to a boiling point. He needed his words, but his brain wouldn't work. Everything was locked up inside him and wouldn't fall into place. "No, please?" he begged, uncaring of his pride.

"Everything is jumbled in my head and my tongue doesn't want to work, so I'm not good at expressing myself right now. I need you to stay. Please sit back down." Omen heard the fear in his voice. He couldn't stop. "Please don't go."

Keegan's chest expanded. He looked resigned. "Okay, sweetie. If you calm down, I'll stay. As a matter of fact, let's turn you on your side and get that blood pressure down." He helped Omen roll over. Omen immediately felt better. Keegan rearranged his pillows.

"You shouldn't be doing that. You're not a doctor."

At his mom's outburst, Keegan smiled but didn't look her way. "Shut the hell up, Nancy. Are you okay?"

A chuckle escaped Omen. His mom didn't know Keegan. She hadn't met anyone like him. If she wanted to budge him, she'd have to fight. "Much better because you're here. I love you." Omen held tight to Keegan. He wasn't ready to risk letting go.

"I love you too. Do you need anything?"

Omen's neediness wouldn't abate. "Just your promise you won't go."

To his surprise, Keegan kissed him. His warm lips brushed Omen's, bringing the calm he required.

Damn, he missed the way Keegan's lip piercings felt when they brushed his lips. "If you're here, I'm here. We'll get through this."

Omen wondered if Keegan meant only his illness, or if he meant all their problems. The break up. His mom. All Omen's transgressions. He prayed it was all the above. Life meant nothing without Keegan. If he got better and Keegan never spoke to him again, then Omen had lived for nothing.

KEEGAN HAD NOT ONCE CONSIDERED PUNCHING an old lady before today. His rage was bottomless. Omen's doctor had emphasized that Omen needed to stay stress free, yet she was determined to start shit. No doubt telling the woman to shut it hadn't helped Omen's numbers, but Keegan couldn't take anymore. He would stay for Omen, but Nancy would have to stop. Keegan wasn't good at staying silent while being walked on.

Omen had told Keegan he loved him several times before today. This was the first time with a witness. Inside, Keegan tried beating back the hope and happiness. His emotions refused to budge. He loved Omen—past deeds and all. Keegan needed to be here, helping his man. He stroked Omen's arms and hands, trying to soothe him.

"You should try to sleep, baby. That'll do you the most good. Your body needs rest." To his surprise, the chair he'd been sitting in moved closer, making it where he could sit and hold Omen's hand. Keegan flashed Nancy a grateful smile before going back to trying to put Omen to sleep.

"You look beautiful."

Keegan shook his head at Omen's stubbornness. "Close your eyes."

Finally, Omen did as told. His eyes slipped closed. Keegan's gaze never wavered from the man's face. There was a slight difference in the left and right side. Damage from his stroke. It took nothing from Omen's beauty. He looked tired and dehydrated. Yet, he was still the sexiest man Keegan had ever seen. Keegan missed watching Omen sleep. He must've spent hours of his life in the past staring at Omen and dreaming of a life they'd never have. Keegan used to watch him in the mornings. He'd fantasize Omen would open his eyes, smile, and say something sweet about how he wanted to see Keegan's face first every day. Instead, Omen would always wake up, look slightly panicked, and rush away. Omen had only loved him when the sun was down. Every other second of the day, Omen had lived in fear of being outed.

Keegan swallowed down the hurt. He didn't know why he always did this to himself. Choking on the past helped no one. Wallowing wouldn't change anything. It only served to punish him over and over again for taking a chance and losing.

Omen's eyes shot open. The panic was back in his eyes, crushing Keegan's soul. Then, his gaze landed on Keegan. His face softened. He took an audible breath. "I dozed off. My brain did something crazy—like it forgot for a moment you were here, and I panicked. I can't lose you ever again, Keegan. You're my person. I don't want to wake up without you."

It was like he'd read Keegan's mind. Keegan floundered under the shock. He'd never considered what he would say in return if he ever got his wish. His mouth didn't seem to need his brain. It moved without permission. "You're my person too. Go to sleep. You don't have to worry about losing me. I'm always here, waiting." Fuck. It was true. No matter what shitty thing Omen pulled, Keegan was always hanging on, waiting for Omen's next trick to fix them. He was hopeless. Keegan didn't relax again until Omen slept peacefully. The moment his spine molded to the chair, Nancy struck.

"He's asleep. You can go."

Keegan drew a deep breath. Never in all his years had he been so exhausted by anyone in such a short amount of time. "For the love of... has this whole episode taught you nothing?" Keegan tried sticking to a stage whisper, hoping he didn't wake Omen. "Life is short. Anything can happen at any moment, and you won't get a chance to take your hate back. Is that what you want? Are you trying to alienate your only son? Because from here, it looks like you're risking everything for nothing. He can't change who he is, and he shouldn't have to earn the love of his mother. That should be freely given."

"I love my son."

"Then act like it," Keegan shot back. "Sit down. Be quiet and support his happiness. That literally costs you nothing."

Nancy's icy blue stare moved over his features. Her disdain could be felt like a physical touch. "What does your mother think of all this?"

Keegan flashed her a smile that felt evil even to him. "She thinks I'm wasting myself on your son."

"What's wrong with my son? Anyone would be proud to have him."

"You're what's wrong with your son," Keegan said, refusing to back down now that she'd started things. "My mom doesn't want me to have to sit through moments like this, but I choose to anyhow, because—despite your thoughts on the matter—I love Omen."

Keegan's shoulders relaxed when five minutes passed in silence. He knew it was too good to last. He was right.

"He said you were just a friend."

"Well, he says a lot of stupid things."

"That's true," Nancy said, taking him by surprise. "I used to get called to the school at least once a week for something he'd done or said. He liked to accuse his teachers of promoting a fascist system."

A snort escaped Keegan. "He said you were a hippie. How does a hippie turn gay hater?"

She rolled her eyes at Keegan's question. "I don't hate anyone. Everyone's always looking at him, judging his every move. There's not a decision Omen makes that doesn't land on the front page of gossip magazines. Now he'll be there with you. People will hate him and say mean things. No parent wants that for their child."

"People hate him and say mean things now for

no reason whatsoever. At least he'll have me to stand with him."

Nancy's shoulders fell along with her defenses. She looked five years older. "But you're so young."

Keegan chuckled. He couldn't stop himself. "Your son is famous. I have a feeling, even if he hadn't fallen for me, you would've had to deal with someone younger than him. At least I'm settled. I own my own business and don't need him at all, except that I love him and need him more than words can say."

With a shake of her head, Nancy looked away. Keegan wasn't sure what the gesture meant. Not that it mattered. He wasn't going anywhere. If Omen wanted him gone, he'd have to climb from the bed and toss Keegan out himself. Otherwise, Nancy would have to deal. As long as Omen was here, Keegan would be too. They were in this together.

A BEEPING NOISE startled Omen awake. Without opening his eyes, he called out for Keegan. "Eat your snack, baby."

"I can't believe you still have that alarm set on your watch."

Omen's eyes blinked opened. Keegan sat in a chair beside the bed, eating a pack of crackers. For a moment, confusion owned Omen. Everything rushed back to him at once. The stroke. His hospital stay. Losing Keegan. Yet he was here, and some part of Omen had known he would be.

"When it goes off each day, I know what you're doing. I know it's dumb. Sometimes, there're thousands of miles between us. I might not know exactly where you are or who you're with, but I know what you're doing. There's been many times that hearing that alarm was the only thing keeping me sane." His gaze skirted away. He didn't mind showing his heart, but Omen wasn't sure it was welcome. They were alone. "Where did Mom go?"

"I convinced her to go to a hotel and get some sleep."

Omen let that detail sink in. He couldn't imagine his mom letting anyone talk her into leaving, especially someone she'd been adamant about in her disapproval. "That's good."

Keegan nodded. "Seventy-two is no spring chicken. She needs to think of herself."

All Omen could do was blink. Things were... odd.

Keegan wasn't finished. "We took a chance and

went down to the cafeteria for dinner while you were sleeping. Luckily, you didn't budge. I worried with all the nurses coming and going, you'd wake up and think I left."

Omen nodded. "Like the last time we were together."

After setting his crackers aside, Keegan moved the chair closer. He stacked his hands on the railing and set his chin on his hands. Keegan held his gaze. "You're supposed to be staying stress free."

Damn, he loved Keegan's eyes. It hit him. Keegan was makeup free. Mostly. There was a hint of light eyeshadow and possibly some clear gloss on his lips. Otherwise, his adorable freckles were showing. "You make my heart skip beats."

Keegan shook his head, but his full lips curled into a smile. "Tell me what you need. Do I need to call a nurse to help you to the bathroom?"

Actually, yes. He did need that, but they were alone. Omen also needed some answers. "Why did you do it? I woke up, and you were gone."

"I'm stupid," Keegan said, taking him by surprise. "My mind got the best of me. You said you'd done an interview, so I searched *Metal Today* and got zero results. I thought you'd lied... again."

"It was with *Today's Metal,*" Omen said, interrupting.

"Yeah, I gathered that when they called the shop and left a message." Keegan visibly swallowed. He glanced away. "I could've lost you and that would've been my last memory. For the rest of my life, I would've known I left without saying a word—too scared to just ask. I would've listened to that message, learned you were telling the truth, and it would've been too late to take it back." Keegan's gaze moved back to his. There was so much pain in Keegan's eyes, it tightened his throat, threatening to choke him. "I'm not ready to lose you."

Real life pressed on his brain, trying to break him. So far, they hadn't found a definite cause for his stroke. Without that information, he was helpless against another one striking him down at any moment. Maybe next time, he might not be as lucky. "I need you to know something," Omen said, scrambling to say the things he wanted Keegan to hear. "I'll never be ready to leave you." The admission hurt. His eyes burned. He blinked, trying to clear his vision. "If I die tomorrow or fifty years from now, I need you to understand I haven't had enough time with you. It'll never be enough time with you."

Keegan came to his feet and lowered the rail. He buried his face against Omen's neck. With Keegan's weight pressing him to the bed and his breath fanning against Omen's skin, the fear set in. He held on to Keegan, soaking in his strength. His body shook. He hadn't let himself look at the situation too closely before now. In Keegan's hold, he realized how close he'd come to losing everything. Omen had always believed he had plenty of time. He could fix things later. Now he wasn't so sure. The thought of dying or losing Keegan for good; he wasn't ready. "I'm sorry I didn't give you the relationship you deserve. I'm sorry I failed us."

Keegan sniffed, making Omen realize he was crying. His heart shattered. Only a true bastard would make Keegan cry. Keegan leaned away and swiped at his eyes. They were red rimmed, which only made them more beautiful. "You'll just have to spend the rest of your life making it up to me."

He would. If Keegan let him. Omen would spend every second, every breath, trying to make up for the year he'd done nothing except take. He would fix them.

SIX

EVEN THOUGH HE UNDERSTOOD WHY CERTAIN tests were necessary, Omen was tired of eating water from a spoon to prove he could feed himself. He was equally tired of getting shots in the stomach, telling everyone what the clock says, and going from sitting to standing to prove that he could. The worst part was the no sleep. Everyone around him set off the alarms on their beds all night by getting up without a nurse's assistance. Between the fucking beeping and nurses coming in and out of his room all night, he never got any sleep.

"Once you make it through this final round of tests, you'll get to go home."

The way Keegan smiled at the nurse's

announcement had Omen focusing solely on him. In fact, Keegan's being there made the whole damn ordeal worthwhile.

"Walk to me."

Omen leaned on his cane and headed that way. "Be there in a sec." It was getting easier. At first, he'd had a little trouble due to his blood pressure medicine being too strong. It had made him lightheaded. Between that and the slight numbness on his left side, he'd nearly fallen a few times. Now he just had to remind himself to use the cane for its purpose. Let it do its job.

"Once you get here, you can kiss me."

That was enough motivation for him. "Give me my prize," Omen demanded the second he reached Keegan's side.

"Make him bend over for it," the nurse said, keeping her tone professional. "Let me see he won't fall over."

Keegan tilted his chin up and waited. This was one task Omen knew he could do. He bent and pressed his lips to Keegan's.

"There's my sexy superstar," Keegan whispered against his mouth.

Omen's chest tightened with love. Keegan hadn't left his side for more than a few hours at a time. Not once the entire time he'd been there. Detroit and Payne had flown in the day after Keegan arrived. They'd ensured Keegan had everything he needed so he wouldn't need to leave Omen's room more than necessary. The pair had also made sure Omen's mom had gotten home safely. To his surprise, she's deemed him in good hands with Keegan and handed over the reins. Omen had never thought he'd see the day. He was certain it didn't hurt that she'd been more than a little taken with Detroit.

"Take a seat. Let's run through these cognitive tests one more time. After that, we'll go through your after-care instructions, and you'll be on your way. Are you excited?"

At the blonde woman's question, Omen nodded. "I'm ready for my own bed." It was a complete lie. He wasn't ready for anything. He'd worked with the same nurse every day on weekdays, and he couldn't recall her name. It was the little things like that he didn't know how to handle. Then, there were the big things—like losing Keegan. Once he was home, Keegan would go back to his apartment and his life. Omen wasn't mentally prepared. Still, he did his best on every question, repeating back numbers, guessing the date, and trying to recall what he'd seen people doing in pictures.

Keegan sat quietly at his side through it all. The moment they were alone again, Keegan struck. "I think I should stay with you for a few days, until you're settled."

Omen had seen this coming. Keegan had been dropping hints for days. At first, he'd been thrilled, but the more he thought about it, the more he realized some things. "You have a shop to think about."

"I can figure out something."

He hated this. "Baby, I don't want you to have to figure something out. You've always been proud of that shop. I can't let you keep it closed any longer for me. Cabot found me an assistant. I'll be okay."

"Oh." Keegan dropped his gaze to his lap. He swiped his hands on his thighs. "I'm glad you have a plan."

Omen wanted to scream. He also wanted to beg Keegan to come home with him, but Omen knew where he'd gone wrong before. When he'd woken up alone in that hotel in California, he'd been resigned, because he should've known it would happen. From the very first time he'd set eyes on Keegan, he'd made all the same mistakes. Keegan filled him with so much lust and longing, his mouth would move, spilling whatever it took to convince Keegan to touch him. It didn't matter if it was lies, as long as it ended with Keegan beneath him. Being with Keegan had always been about Omen's happiness. It was Keegan's turn. This time, it had to be about Keegan or it was only a matter of time before Omen lost him again.

"May I take you to dinner tomorrow night?"

At his question, Keegan met his stare. His expression screamed confusion, but he still nodded. "I'd like that."

Even to Omen, his smile seemed over the top at Keegan's acceptance. He knew Keegan didn't understand. Omen was set on winning him. The right way. The way he should have done the first time. He wanted to be worthy.

TO KEEGAN'S IRRITATION, Omen had a driver take him home each night after their dates. Keegan couldn't stop trying to puzzle it out. It wasn't like they'd just met. There was this deep-seeded fear inside Keegan that they were only temporary. He needed Omen to soothe it away with his touch. But each night, after an extremely heated kiss at Keegan's back door, Omen always left him to head inside alone. To be fair, Omen couldn't make it up Keegan's stairs yet, but Keegan wasn't stupid. His stairs weren't the problem. For whatever reason, Omen didn't seem to want more from Keegan. He wasn't sure if Omen was still recovering and not ready, or hell, maybe they weren't even really back together. It was odd. No matter the reason, all Keegan could do was wait and let the chips fall where they may. He hated every second, especially since the rest of his life was falling apart around him.

The bell jingled above the shop door, pulling Keegan from his thoughts. He'd been ridiculously busy since people learned of his relationship with Omen. The public curiosity chafed, especially since most people only came to gawk and not to buy. He'd never seen lower profits. Keegan's stress level was through the roof. He'd rather have Omen than steady business, but damn. Things weren't good. A woman headed for the counter. He couldn't see anything but the top of her head over the two huge vases of flowers she carried. She set them on the counter, looking out of breath.

"Are you Keegan Bordelon?" At his nod, she smiled. "These are for you."

Keegan eyed the flowers. "Thank you."

With a tiny wave, she left him alone to marvel

over the bright bouquets. One was simple. Two dozen long-stem red roses. Classic and beautiful. The other was an explosion of color. Pink and yellow roses mixed with several lilies and some flowers he couldn't name. They were beautiful. There was only one card.

Keegan flipped it open.

Roses to represent my love. Bright colors for the happiness you've brought into my life.

Keegan couldn't stop staring at the words. He needed to hear Omen's voice. He snatched up the phone and called. If a customer needed anything. They could wait.

"Hello?"

"So, someone sent me flowers," Keegan said, fighting a smile and not bothering with hello. "Since there's no signature, I'm hoping they're from you. It's possible that's only wishful thinking, though." Keegan bit his bottom lip and held his breath. His cheeks hurt from trying not to smile like an idiot.

"I didn't sign the card?" Omen sounded confused. "Fuck. I'm sorry. It's like my brain doesn't want to work right anymore." The aggravation in Omen's voice had Keegan's smile slipping away. "I'm sorry."

"Stop apologizing. I knew they had to be from you."

Omen blew out a breath. It sounded loud across the phone. "Do you like them?"

Keegan stroked the petal of one of the lilies. "They're beautiful. I'm leaving them on the counter in the shop. That way, everyone can see I'm spoiled."

"I miss you."

A lump formed in Keegan's throat. "I miss you too. Can I see you after work?"

"Hmmm, let me think about it." Keegan smiled at Omen's playful tone. "Okay, I've thought about it. I've already arranged for a car to pick you up at six. There's more to your gift."

"I can't wait." Keegan had never meant anything more.

"Me either. I love you."

Even though he was alone, Keegan still dropped his gaze to the counter, as if trying to hide his happiness. "I love you too."

"See you at six."

"I'll be ready." Keegan couldn't wait to thank Omen properly. His heart screamed for Omen's kiss. With all the current bullshit in his life, Keegan was convinced he wouldn't truly be happy again until he had it.

OMEN HAD every intention of taking Keegan out to dinner, the same as he'd done almost every night since he'd gotten home. Tonight, he felt like someone had kicked his ass. Even though he'd learned there didn't need to be a reason anymore, his level of exhaustion still seemed odd. He felt like he could sleep and sleep, never waking. His eyelids itched with exhaustion. Each step he took was like through quicksand. His new assistant, May, had driven him to pick up Keegan. Afterward, she'd fetched them something to eat before leaving for the night. As horrible as he felt physically, guilt was kicking him mentally times ten. Keegan deserved to be showed off to the world. Omen was just so damn rundown.

"If you want to go out, we can." Omen knew he was repeating himself. It was easily the fifteenth time he'd made the claim.

Keegan sighed. Loud. He knew he made Keegan crazy, echoing the same words over and over again, but he needed Keegan to know this wasn't like last time. He wasn't hiding. "You're allowed to be tired. For fuck's sake, I'd rather stay in and let you get the rest you need. In fact, I'm pretty damn sure I've suggested we stay in every night since you came home. You're the one who's insisted we go out."

Even with Keegan's constant assurances, Omen still felt like shit. Keegan looked sexy as sin tonight and Omen was this old man who needed to stay in. "But you're all dressed up."

Keegan glanced down at himself. His pale-yellow shirt and white crop pants suited him perfectly. He met Omen's stare, looking confused. "I'm not dressed up," Keegan argued. His expression said Omen needed to stop before Keegan snapped. "If you remember, I've told you before, I dress for me." As Keegan made the claim, he straddled Omen's lap. He wrapped his arms around Omen's neck. These were Omen's favorite moments, sitting cuddled on his couch.

Omen's arms encircled Keegan, hauling him tighter against him. "Whoever you're dressing for, I'm a lucky bastard. When I set eyes on you tonight, I couldn't believe you were coming home with me."

Keegan stole a small kiss. His expression turned wicked. "By the way, I thought you said you have a gift for me."

"Did I?" He loved teasing Keegan.

"Yep. I clearly remember hearing that on the phone earlier."

"I'd give it to you, but you're sitting on it."

Keegan's face brightened. "Yay! That's my favorite thing of all time."

Omen laughed at Keegan's playfulness. "Not that. Technically, I'm sitting on it too. It's in my back pocket."

Instead of making it easier for Omen to get to his gift, Keegan somehow shifted closer. Their chests met. All Omen could do was stare at the face of the man he couldn't live without. "You're so gorgeous."

The compliment surprised Omen a little. As much time as Keegan put into his appearance, he never talked about anyone else's looks. He noticed other things about people. Their laugh or their intelligence. "Thank you."

Keegan smiled. "Why do you say it like that? You sound like you don't believe me."

"Maybe I don't. You should convince me."

Keegan touched his forehead to Omen's. "You have amazing eyes. They're intense. You make people want to look away and never stop staring at the same time." There was something about Keegan's voice. He almost sounded sad. There was a hint of something in his tone.

"Are you okay?"

Keegan nodded, squishing their heads together

with the motion. Even with his reassurances, Omen kept rubbing Keegan's back. He wanted to soothe him. "I just—" Keegan's cellphone rang, interrupting him. "Dang. Hold that thought," Keegan said, crawling from his lap and going for his bag. He checked the face. "It's the alarm company." He answered. "Hello?"

A call from his alarm company couldn't be good. Omen tried reading his expressions as he spoke.

"No. I'm not there. Yeah. Go ahead and send the police. I'll head that way. Thank you." Keegan slid the phone back in his bag. "The alarm is going off at the store. I have to get over there."

Omen pushed to his feet, using his cane to help. "Let me get my keys and you can drive us over there. That'll be faster than waiting for a car."

"Sounds good." Keegan worried at his bottom lip. "I don't really have anything of value, but I also can't afford this shit right now," Keegan said as he headed for the door.

He hadn't said a word about any money issues. The comment caught Omen off guard. "Hopefully, it's just some homeless person setting it off by mistake. Maybe we can get Micah to come clean up our town too."

"He could do it." The humor in Keegan's voice

took some pressure from Omen's chest. It seemed like, since the stroke, every bit of stress—no matter how small—choked the life from him. He was incapable of handling anything anymore. But he could power through anything for Keegan.

Omen watched Keegan as he drove. His face was tight, making Omen wonder how long he'd been silently stressing while Omen had been oblivious. Maybe not oblivious as much as too sick to notice. Flashing blue lights pulled Omen's attention toward the building as they parallel parked in front of the shop. One of the two large windows was busted out, and the door was gone. That was the damage he could see from the outside.

"Fuck," Keegan cursed, leaping from the car.

Omen's cane and overall uselessness drove him insane as he fought his way from the car. By the time he made it to the door, Keegan was already inside talking to the police. Inside was a horrible mess. Considering Keegan had an alarm, and they'd headed there as soon as it sounded, whoever had done this had still managed to set fire to an entire rack of clothes and rip another to shreds. Omen hovered outside the doorway, listening in while trying to stay out of the way.

"The voodoo shop across the street has a

gazillion cameras. I'll go over tomorrow and ask Baptiste if they caught anything."

The officer nodded along before handing Keegan a card. "We can't watch the place all night. You'll have to get someone over here to secure the front." The guy sounded like a real dick, considering Keegan was standing in center of the destruction of his life.

"I'll call someone and have them board up the windows," Omen offered, pulling out his phone and moving out of earshot to do just that. Within ten minutes, he had someone on their way and the police were already loading up to leave. He'd expected them to be there awhile, but apparently not. Omen stood outside what was left of one of the two windows.

Keegan turned in a circle, eyeing everything. "Well, I'm guessing the hate-filled graffiti on the walls explains why this happened."

"Hate-filled graffiti," Omen echoed, casting a look around. He moved to step over the broken glass and into the building when a sign hanging on what was left of the window caught his attention. He froze. His gaze moved Keegan's way. "Um, why is there a for sale sign in your window?"

Keegan didn't look his way. "Do we have to talk

about this now, while I'm standing in the rubble of my life?"

"Yes," Omen said, unrelenting. "This is where you work and live. Why is it for sale?" That seemed like something Keegan would've mentioned.

Keegan scrubbed his hands through his hair. His gaze moved Omen's way. He looked resigned. "Well, first I nearly depleted my savings with a trip to California. Which I didn't think would be a big deal because I knew wedding season was right around the corner. Then, you had a stroke and I've been here and there and everywhere in between, trying to make everything work." Keegan's voice got higher with every word. "And then, I got hit with an astronomical tax assessment and I can't do it. I won't be able to do it. Like everything else in my life, I've failed at this."

Omen didn't know how to react. Keegan had been all smiles when they were together. He hadn't let on not once that anything was wrong. "Why didn't you say anything? I would've taken care of this."

A tired-sounding laugh escaped Keegan. "You've been a little busy almost dying on me. I didn't want to put any extra stress on you. Plus, this isn't your problem. It's mine."

The shock was quickly wearing off as it transformed into anger. "Anything that happens to you is my problem. I'm your team, Keegan. We're an us. If it happens to you, it happens to me."

"Does it?" Keegan said, sounding unsure. "I mean, we've only been back together for like half-a-second. Hell, I'm not even one-hundred-percent sure we are back together most of the time, since beyond the occasional kiss, you don't seem interested in even touching me."

Damn, Omen couldn't win. "I was trying to go slow, so you'd know I want you for you. That I'm serious about us." Keegan looked ready to break. Omen softened his tone. "Where did you even plan to go? This is your home."

Keegan waved his arms in a gesture somewhere between a shrug and helplessness. "I mean, hopefully, I'll make at least a little something from the sale, but Detroit said I could stay with him."

"In California?" Even Omen heard the outrage in his voice.

"You'll be better soon." The way Keegan made the claim broke Omen's heart. He'd never heard so much pain in Keegan's voice, and he'd done a hell of a lot to hurt Keegan in the past. "Soon, you'll be back to recording and touring. You'll have your regularly scheduled life back, and I'll be nothing again. Your friends will remind you that everything you do reflects on them, and you'll be gone. I don't have any friends here, Omen. It's just me. Once this place is gone and you're gone." He shrugged, looking lost.

"Has loving me been that hard?" Omen couldn't stop the hurt from sounding in his voice if he tried. The fact that Keegan had kept his problems from him piled on top of his life. The stroke. The idea he might never perform again. Losing Keegan over and over again. It was too much for one person. "I get that I hurt you by not telling anyone about you and I'm sorry. I'll never stop being sorry, but I know that I was still good to you. You can't stand here and say you didn't know every day that I love you. Every day. But now, I'm just some guy you can't trust. Someone temporary until you start a new life. I'm not okay with that." Omen wanted to be angry, but honestly, he was just tired. He shoulders fell. "You can't stay here tonight. Go get what you need. I'll be in the car when you're ready to leave." He started to turn away when another thought hit. "Oh, FYI, here's your gift." He pulled an envelope from his back pocket. Keegan reached for it, even though he didn't look like he wanted to touch it. Without looking back, Omen made his way to the car. Keegan would come home with him or he wouldn't. His heart hurt too much to care.

———

WORDS STUCK in Keegan's throat as he watched Omen walk away. Even angry and hurt, Omen didn't intend to leave him. They were both stressed out and snapping at each other. Keegan opened the envelope Omen had given him and unfolded the pages.

Keegan,

After you left me in California, I spent one more night. For hours I sat by the window, staring at the view and seeing nothing but your face. I let all the memories of us that I'd shoved aside flow over me. As I sat there, all the pieces of us fell into place. I realized you're my home, and if I couldn't come back to you, then I'd be homeless.

Keegan chuckled. "Always so poetic and dramatic."

I decided I wouldn't date again. Maybe that seems extreme. It's also possible I would've changed my mind someday, but I doubt it. You're the one for me. Being with anyone else wouldn't be fair to anyone involved. It always surprises me when I think back on the night we met because so many things happened that never do. I got chased by a mob of fans in my hometown. You didn't ask for my autograph, a selfie, or call the police when I commandeered your shop. I couldn't take my eyes off you—a man. Everything just snapped into place, and now I see that night for what it was. Fate. From the moment we were born, we were meant to meet that night at that exact spot. No matter what turns our lives took, or if we were in different bodies, or other professions, we would've still found each other that night. I believe that with every fiber of my being. Since I realized that, I can't stop thinking about it or you. You've helped make me. You've inspired me and motivated me. Without you, I'm nothing. To that end, you deserve part of your creation. My lawyer drew up the pages attached. The song I wrote for you released a week ago. Starting next month, you should see the royalties from it appearing in an account I set up for you. Now some of my words belong to you—literally. The rest of me, well, all I can do is hope that you'll take pity on me and keep me. I'm a little broken and tired now. Maybe not all of me works like it used to, but I'm yours. — Omen

Keegan sniffed, trying not to cry. Omen was music. For him to give Keegan a song, it was exactly like he'd cut out a piece of his soul and handed it to Keegan. And here Keegan was, treating him like he

119

was temporary, just as Omen accused. He re-folded the pages and headed upstairs. Keegan moved slow as he gathered his things. Instead of packing an overnight bag, he grabbed his luggage. He stuffed as much as he could into each piece before locking them together so he could take them in one trip.

By the time he made it downstairs, there was already someone boarding up the place. Keegan swallowed hard. Omen had been right in all his accusations. Keegan had known he was loved. Every day. That hadn't been the problem. The problem was that they'd been so deeply in love that Keegan wanted more. He wanted to be the man Omen came home to, and he'd wanted the world to know it. Keegan had gotten greedy. Now he understood pain like he never had before. The torture of living without his soul. He was so terrified of losing Omen that he'd been shielding part of himself and refusing to believe they were real. That was over. He was doing what he should've back then.

At the car, Keegan opened the back door and shoved his luggage inside. He didn't look Omen's way until he was settled behind the wheel. Omen had the seat reclined and his eyes were closed. There were dark circles under his eyes and face was pale.

Keegan worried sometimes Omen would never be well again. Keegan would love him either way.

Keegan brushed Omen's hair away from his face. Omen didn't budge. His skin felt like ice. Panic slammed into Keegan, forcing his heart into his throat. Keegan shifted to his knees and leaned across the console.

"Omen." He lightly patted his face.

Omen's eyes shot open. "What's wrong?"

Keegan dropped his face to Omen's chest and inhaled. His heart raced too fast to send oxygen to his brain. "Holy shit. You scared the hell out of me." He sucked air, dragging in much needed oxygen along with Omen's scent.

Omen's fingers brushed through his hair. "I'm sorry. Sometimes, I have trouble staying awake. I'm so tired. Why is there like a mountain of luggage in the backseat? Are you moving in?"

Keegan didn't lift his head or sugarcoat it. "Yes."

"Good."

At Omen's response, Keegan smiled against Omen's chest. Omen kept stroking his hair and Keegan's heart finally slowed. Keegan turned his head and pressed his ear to Omen's chest. He needed to hear Omen's steady heartbeat after that scare. Omen cupped his face and used his thumb to trace

Keegan's lips. Keegan kissed his thumb as it passed over his mouth.

"You're not just some temporary guy," Keegan said quietly, needing Omen to know, but not wanting to break the spell.

"I know, baby. That's not really what I think. I believe in us. We're both stressed, and I shouldn't have gotten upset with you while you were already dealing with bullshit."

Keegan shook his head. "I should've talked to you. Instead, I didn't want to dump on you while you're supposed to be resting. We'll get better at talking things out. I believe in us too."

Omen kept stroking his hair. Keegan didn't want to move. He was in the world's most uncomfortable position, slumped over the console with his ass in the air. But he was right where he'd wanted to be for forever, in Omen's arms.

"I'm terrified." Keegan held Omen tighter when he sounded as if his teeth chattered on the confession. He should've known Omen needed him more than he'd let on. Omen was strong. He never seemed to need anyone. "I tried to play my guitar earlier, but I didn't have enough strength or coordination in my left hand. So this might really be it for me. Your song might be my last." His lips brushed Keegan's hair as he made the confession. He didn't stop. "I'm so tired all the time I can't function, much less get turned on. How long will you put up with that? How long will it be before I've lost music and you?"

For a man, that was a legitimate fear. That was the only reason Keegan didn't let the admission piss him off. "We're not about sex. This, what we're doing right now, is what I need and what I've felt cheated out of with you sending me home every night. If you need to sleep all the time, let me cuddle with you while you do. Don't withdraw your affection. Everything else will work itself out. It's this I can't live without."

"We're living together now, so I don't think that'll be an issue."

A chuckle escaped Keegan at the humor in Omen's voice. "True. Once the shop sells, I'll have more time to dedicate to helping you get back your strength. I won't let you lose anything."

Omen shifted, leaving Keegan no other choice but to meet his gaze. "Yet you expect me to just let you lose the store? You love this place."

"Yes. I love this place, and yes, I expect you to just let me lose it. This isn't a decision I came to lightly. It's obvious the building's location ensures that the taxes will only get worse. If I'm not making enough to cover all the expenses, then it's not thriving. I don't want to spend the rest of my life working day in and day out on something that's serving no purpose other than making me work. Who knows? Maybe one day I can start a new business," Keegan said, getting excited. "Oh, maybe I could have my own fashion line. Something that looks vintage but with a modern flair."

"You'd be brilliant." Omen sounded so sure it bolstered Keegan's confidence. He could do anything. "How about this? Let's make a deal. Just hear me out. Let me keep the store afloat for the next two years. I'll hire someone to work it, while you focus on what you want to do. If at the end of two years, you're not happy selling your own designs from the shop or still not turning any sort of profit, you can decide what to do then. We can close the place or use the place for something else. Hell, we could open a music store that sells old records and memorabilia. That's something you rarely see these days."

Every word Omen said sounded amazing. Mostly, because it was obvious, he intended for them to always be together. "Yes. Let's do it."

Omen's smile made any sting to his pride worthwhile. "I love you."

"I love you too. We'll be great. No matter what happens."

They would, Keegan believed. As long as he had Omen, everything else would be just fine.

SEVEN

"Joining us on today's show is heavy metal rock legend, Omen Birch. How are you doing, Omen?"

Omen smiled. Keegan bit back a sigh. He looked so sexy sitting there on stage. "I'm good, Gloria. How have you been?"

"Good. Thanks for asking." The show host beamed. "It's been a while since you've been on the show. You've had some new stuff happening in your life."

"Yeah, lots going on."

Keegan bit his bottom lip, trying to fight back laughter. He loved it when Omen sat in the spotlight.

"Let's start with your interview with *Today's Metal*. That was a particularly spectacular coming out."

A sexy-sounding chuckle fell from Omen's lips. "Yeah, it was time, and Keegan is worth it. He's here, actually. Hiding out over there." The camera swung Keegan's way as Omen nodded toward him. Keegan blushed while trying his damnedest not to hide his face. "Wave at the world, baby." Keegan gave a small wave at Omen's demand. Heat blasted from his face. Thankfully, the camera swung back toward the stage.

"We should get another chair and let your fiancé join us."

Omen glanced Keegan's way. "You can ask, but he's camera shy."

Keegan waved his hands, silently begging for them to move on.

"Awww, well, we'll leave him alone. He's a cutie," Gloria added, making Keegan want to hide his face again. "What everyone here at the station wants to hear about is your recent stroke. That was scary stuff, collapsing while on stage the way you did. How are you feeling these days? Will we see any new music released?"

"I'm doing great. A lot of that is due to Keegan. He works with me every day, helping me regain my strength. I was finally able to ditch my cane three weeks ago. Last week, I started recording again. So you'll definitely see some new music releasing soon."

Keegan chewed on the edge of his thumbnail and absorbed every word. They had been working hard. Omen surprised him daily. He'd never imagined life being so perfect.

Omen had moved on to talking about their upcoming wedding. All Keegan could do was listen and wait. As much as he loved this, Keegan also wanted to get back to their hotel room on the beach. They'd come to California for the interview but were staying to spend time with their friends. The interview didn't take long. Yet it seemed like it took forever to get back to their room. Keegan played with Omen's fingers in the elevator. He couldn't stop touching the man. There was something about the way Omen watched him. It was too intense. In the three months they'd been living together, they'd developed a bond Keegan couldn't describe. They spent nearly every waking hour together. Even though Keegan knew it wouldn't always be that way, he firmly believed they'd needed that unhindered time together.

"I'm sorry."

Omen's apology had Keegan's gaze moving from their entwined fingers to Omen's face. "For what?"

"Your life has been all about me the past three months. Tell me what I can do for you."

A chuckle escaped Keegan. "Are you saying you want me to stop taking care of you?"

Omen's guilt-ridden smile said it all. "No."

"There you go, then. You take care of me. I take care of you. We're not uneven."

Omen held his silence as they stepped off the elevator. He stayed quiet until they were inside their room. "We don't feel even. It feels like I should toss you on the bed and fuck you until you know you're appreciated."

Keegan's breath froze in his lungs. It had been so long. They'd done other things. Less taxing bedroom activities. But Omen's energy was zapped, and—honestly—Keegan had been kind of scared to go farther. He worried about Omen's blood pressure getting too high. Keegan needed Omen around more than he needed sex.

"Are you sure?" Keegan knew it was a stupid question. Omen watched him like he was the man's next meal, and he hadn't eaten in months.

"You should strip," Omen said rather than answering.

Keegan nodded. "I am feeling a bit overheated in these clothes."

Omen didn't smile. Instead, he toed off his shoes and slipped out of his jacket. Keegan hadn't seen Omen in a three-piece suit in a long time. It was sexy. As Omen's hands went to the buttons on his shirt, Keegan turned his back on him and headed for the bedroom. A growl sounded behind him. An evil smile pulled at Keegan's lips.

He looked over his shoulder. "I don't know. Maybe we should go slow."

Before he'd made it five steps, Omen overcame him. His chest hit Keegan's back. Keegan's feet left the floor as Omen lifted him, rushing him to the bed. A loud squeal slash laugh exploded from Keegan. Until his face hit the mattress, and it turned into a moan. Omen tore at their clothes. Keegan let him do all the work. The way Omen's teeth kept sinking into Keegan's skin rendered Keegan useless. When cold liquid swiped up his ass, Keegan tried scrambling onto the bed. Omen kept him trapped in place, bent over the edge.

"No. Right here." At Omen's hard and

demanding tone, Keegan's hips moved. He openly humped the mattress, seeking relief from his raging lust.

"Quit talking about it and fuck me."

Keegan's feet left the floor as Omen's dick stretched him wide. He pumped at the perfect angle. Keegan scratched at the mattress, pushing back against him, needing Omen as deep as he could go. It had been so long. His dick leaked onto the bed, begging. Keegan let Omen's hard thrusts ram him into the mattress, massaging at his cock. Between the friction and the pounding, Keegan was already on edge. He turned his head, needing oxygen. Keegan sucked air, reaching. Winding tighter. His muscles tensed. His gaze landed on the engagement ring he wore. Omen was his. Forever. The pressure tightening his balls and beating at his crown finally broke, sending wave after wave of pleasure racing through him.

"Oh god," Omen cried behind him. "I love you. I fucking love you." At Omen's chant, Keegan's eyes filled with tears. He'd spent over two years of his life loving this man. Many times, it hadn't felt real. More times than not, Keegan had been positive it wouldn't last. Now none of that mattered. Every fight they'd ever had or ever would endure was nothing but fire forging their relationship into steel. They couldn't be broken. This was forever.

KEEP an eye out for the next book in the series, *Sugar Heart*.

ABOUT THE AUTHOR

Please consider leaving a review at the retailer where this book was purchased. Reviews really help with a book's visibility, which ensures I can continue writing. Thank you, Charity.

Charity Parkerson is an award winning and multi-published author with several companies. Born with no filter from her brain to her mouth, she decided to take this odd quirk and insert it in her characters.

*Seven-time Readers' Favorite Award Winner
    *2015 Passionate Plume Award Finalist
    *2013 Reviewers' Choice Award Winner
    *2012 ARRA Finalist for Favorite Paranormal Romance
    *Five-time winner of The Mistress of the Darkpath

Connect with her online:

--Join my street team: facebook.com/TeamCharityParkerson

--Sign up for my newsletter: http://bit.ly/CharityNews

--Website: charityparkerson.com

--Facebook: facebook.com/authorCharityParkerson

facebook.com/TheMenofSin

--Twitter: twitter.com/CharityParkerso